Pra

HIKING UNDERGROUND

● ● ● ● ●

"To read *Hiking Underground* is to enter the slipstream of three equally compelling psyches and to fall into a trance of empathy. Smiley brilliantly evokes the tension between reverie and reality in this deeply humane, beautifully original novel."

– Kate Christensen, PEN/Faulkner award-winning author of *The Great Man* and *The Last Cruise*

● ● ● ● ●

"Smiley keeps the reader of *Hiking Underground* rapt in anticipation, waiting not for some plot conflict resolution, but for the different variations on the novel's theme to converge, which they do, with delightful intricacy. Smiley writes for artists."

– V.N. Alexander, author of *Locus Amoenus*

● ● ● ● ●

"Amy Smiley's subtle triangular rotation evokes a New York City dreamscape that suggests a new, Manhattan version of Louis Aragon's *Paris Peasant*—a vision that Aragon would have found delightful for its freshness and invention, its crisscrossing of myth and wit, its reverence for the city and wonder for nature."

– Jean-Michel Rabaté, University of Pennsylvania, American Academy of Arts and Sciences

• • • • • •

"This remarkable book will hold you in its grasp from the first word to the last. Illuminated by descriptions of ordinary things in urban daily life that suddenly became far more than mundane, the novel is filled with domestic details that echo with deep significance. Its characters live on different planes of consciousness, and Smiley guides the reader into their depths and across their surfaces. Smiley has an uncanny ability to direct readers' attention to the tiny details of how things come into being—from the emergence of a painting from an artist's canvas to the emergence of plants and birds among the concrete blocks and buildings of a city. *Hiking Underground* is an engrossing narrative, original in its conception, and so powerful that it will forever change the way you pay attention to the world around you."

– Emily Martin, author of *Experiments of the Mind: From the Cognitive Psychology Lab to the World of Facebook and Twitter*

HIKING
UNDERGROUND

a novel

AMY SMILEY

atmosphere press

For my father, Jerome Ira Smiley, who taught me about poetry and gardening at the same time.

And for Billy, who inspired this story.

To mothers everywhere, especially my own, the beautiful Eleanor Lewit Smiley, who ever lives within me.

ACKNOWLEDGEMENTS

I wish to thank, first and foremost, my husband, Mark Crispin Miller, under whose caring and critical eye the final manuscript more fully bloomed.

I am grateful to the visual artist Sarah E. Brook for her close reading of the sections of the manuscript related to Emma's art.

My thanks to Emma Parry, agent, who read the manuscript several times and gave me encouragement and guidance.

The perceptive reading of my work by Trista Edwards, my editor at Atmosphere Press, was especially helpful.

My heartfelt thanks to Nick Courtright, CEO and Executive Editor of Atmosphere Press, for believing in the novel and to all the staff who helped bring it to the light of day.

The cover illustration by the photographer, Francine Fleischer, captures perfectly the essence of this work.

Tammy Smiley's support for my writing has sustained and moved me.

Part II, chapter I, "Alice," first appeared as a short story, *Full Moon*, in *Raritan*. It is reprinted here, with their permission.

PART ONE

I. Alice

Was the whole world dreaming, or just one young woman?

That place, where the dream stretches thin and veil-like, had become her room. Was it her room—or anybody else's, for that matter? That shadow—was it something cast out from the dream-world, or was it really there, barely visible against the darkness? She rolled onto her side, then floated up above her bed, the air becoming buoyant between her hip and the mattress as she considered this voluminous tuft, flung on a slant, pale and hovering, arresting her attention, till she relaxed in relation to what was a shadow, only white, outside the order of things, yet not quite disturbing either, at least for the moment, when all at once it furled itself—a visual gasp—and then went silent, hanging in midair, only to unfurl and flutter. This was no bird, though, but an inflated wisp, oddly billowing, writhing, deflating, turning pale, and hovering again. Was it her heart she heard now or the quickening of the shadow? Had her eyes adjusted to the dream light, or was the shadow really brightening, now luminous?

Alice always walked between two worlds, so it was hard to say where one began and the other ended. Most often she could distinguish between them, but when she couldn't, or when her body couldn't, she had to take a moment until things separated themselves out. So now, the wispy shadow was a curtain, rising and falling in an uneven wind; it was morning; and she was slowly coming out of an artificial sleep. And the morning hit her hard, constricting her throat as she tried to swallow when a rush of pain made her break into a sweat. A jagged star was stuck in her throat. She tried to cry out, but it cut again. Right. She remembered. They had warned her that it would hurt, especially right afterward. There was really nothing special about it; she was only one of millions. For three thousand years, inflamed tonsils have been surgically removed. This was a day like any other in the history of a minor procedure. And so, for the weeks after the diagnosis, she did her best to forget. But sometimes, she lay awake admitting to the stuffed animal by her side—a goose with a gentle eye—that she thought it barbaric. They clamp your mouth open, dissect through the tonsils with a scalpel, and then burn them closed. Sort of toasting your tonsils like marshmallows. The wound would scab over and eventually fall away, the doctor explained, trying to reassure her. Fall away? Would she swallow her own wound? Now there's a thought. It was sort of like Hattie, licking her pierced paw for hours after she'd hurt it in the woods. Well, if dogs did it, Alice could too. She would swallow her burnt tonsils and take it like a man, as it were. She wasn't a kid any more, or almost wasn't, never having felt that total independence thing like some of the other students she knew, who had real jobs and paid their own rent well before graduating. But the truth was that a tonsillectomy was simply hell, worse for an adult, in fact, so she must have become one very recently, given how she felt right now, contorted, howling, and all alone in the outpatient wing of the Morristown Medical Center.

Or maybe she wasn't an adult if being one meant "keeping it together", controlling the contortion of her face, the quiver in her voice, the urge to dart away. The only difference between the present and her high school years was that now she didn't want to give herself away. Back then, though, she truly couldn't help it, so it never occurred to her to try, and so she always stayed on the outside of that golden group of girls who ran the world—the ones with the A papers, harmless boyfriends, family vacations. What was the attraction, anyway? It was a pretty boring life and probably not even real. But for all that, it claimed absolute power. Now, at

22, she imagined that those girls, too, had had their share of sorrow. But in the world of that middle-class New Jersey high school, there was a tacit, implacable pressure to not show her real self and, when emotion betrayed her, Alice would just want to disappear. What did real feelings have to do with anything in the blithe exchanges that began with *oh my gosh*, and ended with *what-ev-er*? She would turn her face away, stung by the thought of her father and the fault line running through her family; Heather or Daria would give her one of those cold, quizzical looks that would disjoint her altogether if she didn't jump into the conversation. And yet it was the very thing that made her beautiful, said the first boy who ever loved her—that way she had of expressing what lived inside of her, while others seemed to rove around, staring into cyberspace as they chatted from the sides of their mouths.

That was nice of Mike to say—it was better than nice, it was even vindicating, for about five minutes. But she didn't know *how* to feel superior since they all came from New Jersey, anyway, didn't they? How could those girls be one way and Alice another? Besides, or more to the point, how could something so raw be beautiful unless you held it at a distance, and then was that love? It was more like admiration, and it didn't last with Mike, because she just felt too shitty about herself, so compliments had the effect of making her think he was talking to someone else. But in her innermost reflections, she conceded that there was a sort of veil that seemed to pose itself numbly on everything around her. She never felt quite right in that small town of hers, except with Pam, the one person she could just *be* with, say what she thought, and tell her secrets to. Pam lived on a working farm, one of the last in the region; most of the others had been converted into horse ranches. Not that Alice didn't like horses. At least once a week, she would trek out past Pam's to Millicent's to help out in the stables. When, some two miles off, she smelled the mingling odors of warm hay, horse hair and oats, she would let it all go and race the rest of the way, arriving sweaty and panting with only one thing on her mind: a hug from Juniper—as much as a horse and a girl could hug. Juniper had a look in her eyes that went deeper than anything Alice knew. She could hear her whinnying from the pasture, almost yelling out to her to come, quick! Juniper would trot up to the fence and greet her, stop for a moment, and fix her gaze on the girl, then, having sized her up and taken in how hard it all was, would gently bow her head as near as possible to Alice's own face, their breaths mingling. At last, the horse would get impatient and would give her a familiar nudge, and Alice would jump over the fence and run down the hill in search of a bucket of oats. They would stay together under the same old apple tree for hours, Juniper whisking the flies away with her tail and glancing at Alice, who, settled in the grass, looked out over the hills, unveiled at last.

It was at such a moment, when all seemed well with the world, that Alice had once found herself looking beyond those hills, imagining the city where her life would somehow transpose itself in a matter of weeks, and that just then Rodger was walking up the road, and looking her way. Of course she knew Rodger, or at least of him, but he had graduated high school years before—five was it?—and had maybe even graduated college. She knew little about him—surprisingly little since everyone knew everything about everybody else around there—and as she paused to wonder why this was, he waved, and she waved back, feeling her heart bang around her rib cage like a trapped water balloon. Rodger walked over and smiled, almost shyly, and stayed at her side until sundown, when the cicadas made such a racket that both, finally, had to stop pretending that it wasn't time to go. They'd talked so much that Juniper, who never heard Alice speak more than a few words of affection, wandered off incredulous at all the chatter (and Alice could talk, *and talk*, when she got going), leaving the two to devise a beginning of themselves, each searching, awkwardly, the other's hand and, catching it in a warm grip, fell silent.

Getting to know Rodger had a mystery all its own. Before he came into her life, people, as she knew them, just *were*. But here she was, at the close of the day, for weeks on end, revising endlessly, as the now gentle, now bold, now adept, now reticent young man turned her ideas of manhood inside out. More than anything else, he was just plain competent, seemed to be able to make anything, or make anything work, so building a treehouse in her backyard was accomplished in a matter of days, and she perched there long hours doing her homework. At night, Rodger would join her up there, and they would stretch out on some old blankets with flashlights, in the company of fireflies, and spend the summer nights stargazing and reading Greek stories of the constellations till they passed out. Early in their relationship she found herself bike-riding beside him down the mule path along the canal. Alice went over a piece of glass and popped her front tire; she actually flew headfirst over the handlebars onto the shore, her knees and hands jutting out to break the fall and cut them open on the gravel. Rodger caught her in his arms as she rose, wobbling. He cleaned her up, fixed her tire (who carries around an inner tube?), and had her riding back home in no time, though slightly shaken. For a girl who walked in the world of thick emotion, this was news, and getting to know Rodger became a way for Alice to get to know another part of town, the place where things were possible.

Who was he, though, deep down? It was hard to say, even after all those years. He was not one to dwell on himself, even for a moment, and Alice learned pretty quickly that asking questions that weren't about nature or science or psychology or history—in short, anything *but* him, was completely useless. Rodger was what he cared about, thought about, and did. And for Alice, who considered the intrinsic value of a thing to lie in direct relation to how she felt about it, this represented a whole other way of being, and it modified her own, or at least challenged the emphasis she placed on her inner life. But she would find herself, in the middle of the night, when she longed for Rodger, in the grip of a quiet uneasiness, as she drifted in and out of sleep.

For all his investment in the real world—and by that, he meant his never-ending drive to fix things, bicycles, door hinges, or people in pain—Rodger was nevertheless aware that he was elusive when it came to himself. He stopped short at the threshold of those open doors where Alice wanted him to enter, where she went all the time, seamlessly, or so it seemed, even if she suffered for it. They were trap doors, really, and there was that risk that he would fall through, although he was perfectly confident that, for others, this kind of talk was not only desirable but necessary. As far as his psyche was concerned, Rodger was of the mind that it had a life of its own, and that it would grow and be whole again if he would simply leave it alone. So being elusive was just another thing he was perfectly invested in; neither the breezes of April nor the hot nights of August could persuade him otherwise, as much as he loved Alice, in any season.

Alice, of course, had no access to these meditations of his, and her happiness hinged on the fact that he was simply there, holding her hand, which was proof enough that he accepted her. And acceptance, even at age 22, continued to preoccupy her. It wasn't hard to notice how people subtly edged away when her empathy bore on the everyday, like her terror about a pair of pigeons on the sidewalk. Amanda, who befriended her the day she arrived in the city, gave a soft shrug of the shoulders, dismissing the birds entirely. The female had a broken wing! Those few feet of concrete was all it had left, except for its mate, hovering nearby, approaching every few seconds, then stepping back, looking away, as if searching for some solution. Alice called Animal Control and demanded they come at once, only to be told that they didn't respond to calls about pigeons, the outcasts of the animal kingdom. Years later, walking through the zoo in Tunis, a *pigeon américain* caught her eye as it sat wistfully in its cage, like some exotic cockatoo, wondering, it seemed, how it ended up on the shores of North Africa where the evening smelled of jasmine, when, had it stayed in New York, it would have been just another of those grey flapping things that a child would chase or toss a crumb to every now and then. But at least it would be free! Alice looked around for Amanda, who was across the street at a café window, rolling her eyes and motioning to Alice to come join her. Alice would have put her head down on the table and wept for that bird and its devoted mate, but Amanda's likely impatience checked her impulse. It was a grueling but necessary education, learning to leave things where they were.

What might appear to be excessive sentimentality was actually the stuff of a symbiotic connection: what Alice saw, she experienced, as if it were happening to her. And in a way, it was. If a dog crossed the street with a limp she would feel it in her leg. She comprehended, in her bones, what it was like to be a dog with a limp. She kept those experiences to herself, though; she had enough social anxiety as it was. Rodger, who sensed the subtlest change in mood, noticed the queer look on Alice's face every now and then and silently acknowledged that she had a secret life that might be as tormented as his own. It was a question of approach, he told himself. But approach mattered. As gentle as she was, she pushed him. At times, she thought, he retreated, out of nowhere. She was only trying to have a conversation with him.

The loneliness of the recollection was softened by the billowing curtain, but charred by the fire in her throat. What would an hour, let alone a whole day, bring? This pain was no joke, and she would've gladly told the first person to walk through the door just how bad it was, if only someone would. Finally, a nurse entered with a breakfast tray and a warning not to cry. "You need to give yourself a chance to heal," she commanded, then turned and left the room. Thanks a lot, Alice muttered under her breath, groping restlessly for the sense of completion that had wrapped itself around her during the past four years, and a presence that lingered still, now receding, now returning. The light on the sill went from dull to stark (a cloud must've dislodged itself from the overcast sky). The off-white curtain, billowing with a quiet violence that had roused her from the anesthesia, was, in fact, a ghost: the ghost of Rodger. She called to the nurse who had paused in conversation with a doctor just outside the door and asked if anyone had come to see her as she glanced furtively at the clock, which pointed to eleven when visiting hours began. She didn't take it like a soldier when the nurse reappeared to confirm the obvious, as Alice, barely able to delay the lava-like sob that rose from the base of her throat, smothered her face in the pillow. It hardly mattered anyway, as the nurse was already halfway down the hall, pausing momentarily in someone else's pain.

If he weren't there now, he wouldn't be coming later, at all, ever. She thought they had repaired it, but she had obviously deluded herself: something had snapped last autumn when she went back to New Jersey for the weekend. As she walked into her house, she heard the rattle of dishes and found her mother, Jenna, packing up the kitchen. Jason,

Alice's stepfather, had managed the inconceivable: he had found a new house the very week that Jenna closed on a deal to sell Alice's childhood home. They were moving out and "starting fresh", Jenna explained. Not that Alice didn't want her mother to be happy, but the fervor in her mother's eyes was all she needed to understand that those years with her father would be left behind like a beggar that one passes by, in silence. For all she knew, her father, Hank, was at his desk at that very moment, staring off into space and measuring the gulf between himself and the world around him, full of disgust for family, work, and all the other absurd conventions that pinned him down when what he really wanted from life was adventure. That was gone now, beaten out of him, and it was getting harder to find a reason to go on doing anything at all. Faithfully, once a month, Alice would join him for long walks on the beach, leaving them wind-blown and more alive than usual. She would come away with a taut strand of a bond to that very handsome man who was her father, who, with that painful gaze of his, could never quite take her in, leaving her with that familiar ache of longing and despair.

Alice thought of him protectively as Jenna and Jason dashed around with packing paper, pots and pans, stopping every now and then to tell her something else about the great new house. "Simply beautiful," her mother gushed, "with a cedar fence and acres of land, and you're never going to believe this: *a swimming pool.*" (More like suburban death, Alice thought, only to find herself, a few years later, yelling out "this is heaven," as she dove into its crystal clarity, conscious, even at the moment, of pleasure, and of the radical adjustment she had made.) But it wasn't until her mother mentioned the fence that Alice became aware of how much of an outsider she was. That fence would wind itself around someone else's dream of the perfect family with no fights, no pain, no sorrow, just good cheer, the kind that was Jason's, who probably never wept a day in his life over anything. Her mother deserved a life with such a man—a life where everything came easily. And he obviously loved Alice, or really wanted to, and that had to count for something. But she could never give herself entirely to that new family since a part of her remained in the shadows, beyond the great lawn, uncontained. That was the place, perhaps the only one, where she could join her father.

"It's for you!" she recalled her mother yelling from behind a wall of boxes that almost came tumbling down, but which were steadied by Jason's rapid grasp as Alice leapt for the phone. Rodger always had this soulful way of saying hello, but that day he was edgy, and Alice too was not exactly calm; so they repelled each other from the first without meaning to. Alice choked back the tears and apologized, explaining hurriedly that "everything was uprooting itself," which Rodger didn't understand, or at least didn't care to, just then. He had a lot on his mind. The boys at the shelter had managed to set fire to the basement, and Rodger, who seemed to smell it from the highway on his way to his unbearable job, raced to the old brick building and had it put out in minutes, drenching himself and everyone else with the fire hose that, in a moment of uncanny foresight, he had bought at a local auction, just in case, and which was easily connected to the hydrant a few feet from the basement window.

"So her parents bought a new house," Alice imagined him thinking. "Big, fucking deal."

Rodger was losing patience with Alice's intensity, which he once called "self-indulgent," while he had "real responsibilities" for eight boys who had no desire to follow rules of any kind. Each thread of purpose had been snapped, every bit of trust betrayed, leaving them without a friend or relative to take them in. Rodger was their last hope, or so it seemed, and this put them in a rage, as a last hope would do to anyone. In comparison, Alice's ponderings about herself and her family were beginning to grate on him. As it was, he was losing sleep, fearing that he couldn't be that rock for those boys, and wondering if he, too, would have to abandon them. Alice couldn't entirely censor her own preoccupations, although she did manage to keep them to herself, for the most part, and while she had the distinct impression of wearing a mask, it calmed Rodger momentarily, and they persevered, grasping at each other in their worst moments of self-doubt, and somehow made it through the winter, at times so lovingly that Alice started thinking they would marry by the end of the year, and Jenna thought so, too.

What were those trees on the edge of the park? She strained to make out the shape of the leaves; they shimmered in the flood of light on what looked like a summer morning. But it was only May. Were they beeches? She was puzzled, then apathetic. As if it mattered! But trees did matter, even more than people. Remorseful, she looked away, back toward the darkened hallway where no one was coming. A strange panic gripped her as she realized that it wasn't only Rodger who wasn't there but her mother who was inexplicably late. In the darkest moments, when her father slammed the door for like the hundredth time with a hellish, haunting sigh, Jenna would put aside her own distress and go to Alice standing behind the armchair, frozen in his sudden absence. It was the pain that kept her mother by his side until the end—that empty space of his that she thought she could fill, yet remained outside of it, and enraged, every time he had one drink too many. And yet, for Alice, there was nothing, not even that emptiness of his, that could break her, nothing that could irremediably repress the joy that was hers alone, absolutely singular in its power to bubble over with the wonder of a friend, a horse, a boyfriend, a willow, or whatever else that might, even for a second, seem all that she had ever hoped for, and grip her at the root.

But what could hold her in place now? The emptiness of the room acted on her like a vortex. Where had they gone? She didn't know them! She leaned toward the nightstand in search of the glass of water and groaned impatiently when she realized it was empty. She threw her legs over the side of the bed and got up too quickly, which, although dizzying her, didn't get the best of her. At least she could walk across the room for some water! That act, as insignificant as it was, rid her of the passive anxiety that was swallowing her alive. With a burst of energy, she pulled her backpack off the closet shelf and began gathering her things, bending over for a book here, a comb there. There was no way she was spending the night in that hell-hole with everybody on their backs, yielding to bodily intrusions of every kind, the very antithesis, in fact, of intimacy. The association clutched her swiftly as she remembered Rodger. Her desire rose at the instant, replacing her frailty with balmy, bodily recall. Alice found herself in an uncanny place where Rodger, although absent, held her tight. There or gone, lost or found, had no meaning, and she ceased, finally, to experience her connection to Rodger in those polar terms.

She felt herself grow faint and staggered just as Jenna flew to her side and caught her in a solid hold. Her mother filled the room with that familiar smell of verbena. Alice locked gazes with her and let the tears go. Her mother held her and, sensing the pain, rose to call for the doctor, while Alice wished that Jenna would just sit quietly on the bed and hold her for the rest of the year. The nurse said that the doctor would be by in about twenty minutes and left to fetch some Tylenol with codeine—the only thing that Alice would be allowed to take for the next two weeks.

Jenna, who was a nurse herself, knew that the degree of pain her daughter must be feeling was beyond the reach of ibuprofen and codeine. Her worry grew as she looked again into Alice's face and noted her bloodshot eyes. Jenna began silently calculating how much time off she could take from work, how she could divide it up into half-days here and there throughout the week, and if Gran could spend some afternoons at the house. Out of the question to ask Jason; he was somewhere at the tip of Manhattan, analyzing the investment plan of some big firm or other, his concentration at its keenest—he was known for it—as he readied himself for his final prediction. But her thoughts immediately returned to her daughter who was now in a heap, though anything but limp, from the looks of it, but rather jagged with emotion.

Jenna searched her daughter's face and saw Rodger, or rather his absence, in her eyes. "Maybe he called?" she quickly suggested. In her clouded state, Alice had forgotten about her cell phone. As she reached for her bag, her mother grabbed her arm, startling her. Jenna had meant no harm; she only wanted to remind Alice that cell phones weren't allowed in the hospital. And yet, the mother's aggression, however slight, wasn't lost on Alice, who demanded, in defense of her emotion, that Jenna take the phone outside to see if there were any messages.

"What the hell! I'm sick of them all!" Alice yelled toward the door that her mother yanked shut in haste, in a fit of remorse, for so many things. Jenna returned momentarily with a sorry look, as the only message was the one that she herself had left about running late because of traffic.

Alice felt a rush of shame at the idea that Rodger had left no word or couldn't even be bothered to say he wasn't coming. After all that had passed between them! She knew full well that this was precisely the reason, but in her vulnerable state imagined there was something vicious. Could Rodger intentionally hurt her? She wanted to say something, anything, to Jenna to make up for that surge of anger a moment ago, but she was reduced to silence, and the tears streamed down her face. Aggression and pain broke into the most ordinary—and therefore unpredictable—circumstances, indeed governed families like Alice's despite the real bond between them. They were somehow the prey of forces that made their way inside the two car-garage home: for the girl, it was alienation; for the mother, the imperative of order; for the stepfather, the value of financial success, and for the absent father, rebellion.

"What's this? Does it really hurt so much?" asked the doctor who competently strode into the room. "Little ones cry after a tonsillectomy, but not grown-ups." Alice had no patience for this paternalistic bullshit but, unable to come up with an appropriate snide remark, just gave him a look that said, "You gotta stop." Getting it, an expression of serious-ness spread over his face, but the admonishments kept coming anyway. "Look, I know it hurts, but you're going to have to be tough. The Tylenol with codeine will help (Alice caught her mother's look of exasperation), and in a few days it will be almost bearable." In a few years, more likely, Alice thought, as her mind wandered over to Rodger and life without him. Amazing how this doctor doesn't even have a clue who he's talking to and why the tears and why the pain. If it weren't so hideous, it would almost be funny.

"So take a deep breath, because there's one thing you are *not* allowed to do."

"What's that?" the two women asked in unison.

"Cry. I don't have to tell you that your throat is raw from surgery and that it needs to heal. You're still a teenager"— Alice looked younger than her years—"so chances are you'll feel better in seven to ten days. Your recovery depends on staying hydrated. Crying not only induces dehydration but it makes swallowing even harder than it should be. I highly recommend popsicles, sport drinks, grape or apple juice, milkshakes... absolutely nothing acidic..." Alice tuned him out, but Jenna questioned his instructions in detail and, certain that she understood all of them, asked him to prescribe a stronger medication. "Out of the question. She'll be fine with the Tylenol." As Jenna pushed further, the doctor looked at his watch and fled to the next bedside.

"I bet *he* never had *his* tonsils out," Jenna blurted out while he was still in earshot. "She has my back," Alice thought with relief.

The nurse returned with a cup of apple juice and, after a brief examination, said Alice could go home as soon as she was ready, but not without her own admonishments: "Even if you feel sick, you must force fluids." Alice cringed at the thought and looked away as Jenna signed the release papers. Wishing Alice a speedy recovery, the nurse bustled out of the room as if the world depended on her clinical efficiency. Alice shrugged impatiently with the whole hospital scene and thought of Amanda, hoping she would come out for a visit, yet fearing that her friend would have little tolerance for her pain, and then of Pam, wondering if she were back in New Jersey and why she hadn't been in touch those past few months.

Later, in her own room, in her own bed, Alice had little memory of the ride home from the hospital, except that it was a weirdly beautiful day. It made her realize that she had been so preoccupied with school and seeing Rodger that she hadn't been 'round to see Juniper that whole year, and she felt bad about neglecting the horse. She hadn't called Millicent in ages, even just to say hello as she usually did and, rising to look for her cell phone, thought better of it. To talk was excruciating, and she might burst out with something incomprehensible. She went to the closet for a change of clothes and saw her old purple jersey beckoning, like so many memories in her room, and that she always seemed to uncover in a sort of a daze as she walked through that space which had always been so foreign and remote, even though her things from the old house hung all about the walls. The old house had receded into some bottomless place from which she pulled up shreds from time to time. The memory-soaked clothes had a strange quality about them, real and unreal, like Rodger's absence. Alice caught herself looking out the window and *saw* him turn into the driveway, a vestige of a long reality, suddenly interrupted by this ghastly daydream of herself without him.

Naked, she felt naked in the quiet of her room, and threw on her jersey, amazed that it still fit. Good old number 22. Of all the sports—and she went out for all the teams (where she found the energy was beyond her mother, who was relieved but saddened by the sweat-drenched uniforms that Alice threw into the hamper almost every night of the week, the remains of the game signaling an exhausted distress)—her favorite was field hockey. She played Center—bounding over the field, always beaming at her own ability to master that runaway ball with a jerk of her hockey stick, the leader of that squad of girls who backed her every move... like when she smacked it over to Claudia, who caught it with a grateful smile (Alice had worked her hard to help her make the team), and, as they neared the goal, cocked her head to signal she was going to fire it back, and Alice lunged for it, and it looked like was she going down, and everyone gasped—she could hear her father in the bleachers, and she would not disappoint him, so she caught herself, stayed on her feet, shot out her stick and whacked the ball into the net—the winning goal. "YES!" she heard him scream and saw his fist fly high—the only time that he ever showed such pride, and it made the whole goddamn game worth it. She ran to him and he caught her in the bear hug she always longed for, and for once, forgot everything else.

That was the first night in a long time that her parents seemed to get along, just like old times, and so Alice, who had made it happen, played with uncommon determination every day until the sun went down, in the October glow of reddened leaves. The jersey still smelled of those cool nights when Alice walked home from practice, hot and sweaty, her shoulders always tensing as she turned up the driveway, hoping all was well. More often than not, her father's car was gone, and her mother would meet her with the false cheer that she hated more than anything, and she would storm into her room and tear off her uniform.

Alice took off the jersey, threw it on the closet floor, and slammed the door, angry with this younger self who'd hoped so stubbornly that the marriage could be saved. Even now she sometimes caught herself in a vision of her dad returning to the house that was no longer theirs but whose step up to the front door might magically bring it all back. What she missed most of all was the tire swing, the way it lunged out over the dip in the lawn so that a whole valley seemed to open up below and she had but to sway, back and forth, to cross the breadth of it. She reigned over the land for hours, imagining she lived in quite a different world—with girl rulers like Ozma, revered by all for her kindness and beauty. Jenna and Hank had read her the Oz books, all thirteen volumes, and so for two years her world was peopled with the Cowardly Lion, Button Bright, the Shaggy Man, Dorothy, Glinda, and a host of evil characters, each more treacherous than the last, but all of whom would suffer ignominious defeat at the hands of a child. But what Alice loved more than all those victories was Ozma's enchanted mirror, where Alice would imagine she could see her friends in trouble and, in a flash, would rush to their rescue. They so admired her for that power! Alice could still feel herself on the swing, deep in her world, and infinitely content. She laughed aloud at the thought of Hattie, racing around below, barking at Alice to come down already, chasing her back and forth until, tired of her heroic efforts, she got off at last to run around the yard with that big lovable brown dog who'd finally succeed in knocking her to the ground and leap over her victorious. Alice missed that dog with her whole heart. She would never, ever get over losing her. Those eyes, deep and dark, were alive with the mystery of animal knowing as they looked back at you.

Jenna knocked quietly, came in, and, noticing Alice undressed, went straight to the closet to find her something to put on. After all, her daughter was recovering from surgery. Spying the purple jersey on the floor, and as she bent down to retrieve it, she remembered how that very gesture had once ordered her life and how grateful she had been to have something to distract herself from the latest fight with Hank.

"Honey, I thought I heard your cell while I was in the kitchen," Jenna said, turning to throw Alice the jersey, but her daughter was already halfway down the stairs. "Could you at least put some clothes on?" Jenna called after her. Like Alice, she was hoping it was Rodger, but then knew it wasn't, from her daughter's heavy step back up the stairs.

"It was my professor, about the babysitting. She wants to make a schedule. She mentioned that Adam couldn't wait to see me again." Alice crawled into her bed with trembling lips.

"But that's wonderful!" Jenna replied. "Call her back right away. Of course, you can't start until you feel better, but you could at least make a plan."

"Please, mom, I'm in no state! I can't have her hear me like this! What will she think?" And Alice's tears spilled forth anew. No matter how tightly she held her, Jenna understood that she was of little comfort to her daughter, who had this way of crying from the throat, somewhat scratchy and wounded, like an animal in the woods. Then Jenna remembered the doctor's warnings about crying and dehydration, so it was imperative to stop the flood, and Jenna became agitated, which made Alice all the more frustrated. If only she could just sit still and let her cry! Why was that so hard? Jenna rose to get Alice a glass of water, the very thing she should and shouldn't do (Alice was dying of thirst but needed someone to hold on to). It was probably the one thing that Hank knew how to do right: just sit quietly. At those moments, Alice felt they were connected, whether it were true or not. She became all the more impatient and sent Jenna to the store for ices. Alice heard the car door slam and felt bad about pushing her mother away like that. She pulled the sheet up over her shoulder, and in the lonely quiet of the room, sank into oblivion.

There was a tapping, very faint, but she could hear it—, sometimes three taps, sometimes four, then a pause, for a few seconds, or a minute—and it would start again, but more insistent and a little louder, beckoning, agitated, as if someone were out there, in the middle of the night, throwing pebbles at the window, one by one, not to get someone's attention but to break and enter. The objects in the darkened room hung indistinct, yet she could make out something hovering at the sill, barely lit by a piece of dull moon. The tapping got louder, was intolerably loud when she realized it wasn't tapping but pecking—a beak pecking hard at the window. Alice froze in fright. Was it a bird? Why did it want to come in? It was as if the window wouldn't break because it was unnatural for a bird to come inside, yet it was obvious that the bird was in distress... or searching for Alice, to take her somewhere, out and away? Sweating, she got out of bed to look and woke up halfway across the room.

Rain was beating on the window, or was it hail, which explained the sound of pecking at the glass. Alice had been asleep for hours and didn't know the hot blue day had somehow turned stormy. It felt like days had passed, but it was still that very day. This was new to her, this heaviness of minutes; everything was usually so full, or rushed, or carried by anticipation of a class, a trip, a visit. She had no idea how to inhabit this particular world that spun on sluggishly without a purpose, and shrank from it as a child from a dying elder. The queerness of the feeling filled the darkened room as dusk approached. She heard Jason's car pull into the driveway and felt unusual relief; Alice always took his comings and goings for granted but now was grateful for the distraction. "Jason, she's asleep," she heard Jenna whisper.

"No, I'm not, I'm up!" Alice called out and heard her stepfather's answering quick step up the stairs.

"You didn't!" she exclaimed as Jason handed her a fragrant bouquet of lily of the valley. Whenever May came around, Alice would run to the shady pines and ferns, way in the back of the yard, where the tiny white bells, nestled in their two proud leaves, would spring up intoxicating; the scent was so sweet! Such power in so small a thing, such sweetness... and Alice would ponder how a thing so utterly lovely also could be poisonous. She had eaten a small handful of the bells one late afternoon, tantalized by the fragrance, and soon found herself doubled over with pain.

"What a fool. Flowers aren't for eating," she overheard Jenna comment to Jason late that night. Yes, well, a fool she might well be to the end, and preferred it to the careful ways of the world. And she loved the flower all the more in its defense, and in her own. It became a bit of a joke between

Jason and herself, which he didn't overuse, and here they were, gazing at the perfect gift designed to make her laugh and make her glad.

She threw her arms around him, and he beamed but looked concerned—a welcome change from his usual way of greeting her, one that didn't ask to know very much. This time he waited and smiled gently. Jenna waltzed in with a glass of water and a bowl of orange ices, content to see husband and daughter in a moment of affection. It was all she wanted, all she needed, to be content, to feel the happy union of her family.

It came as a surprise, though not entirely, that she was able to love again. Hank had inspired feeling unlike any man in her life. He charmed her entirely as if she were under a spell... something about his gait, the way he moved, and his voice was so sexy. He spoke about things in a way that rattled her, making her question her most basic assumptions about the world. She wanted to think the best of people but was, on reflection, naïve to the point of blindness. She was no coward, that was clear. She could dress the scariest wound, stand by strongly when a patient was in pain, be a constant source of hope to those who needed it most. And she knew that people could hurt each other. Slowly, in time, what once had felt brave in Hank became alien to her, or rather it was his increasing alienation that repelled her; it imbued the world at large and down to his very family, herself first and foremost, but maybe even Alice too. Did she want to be such a mother, one who had to shield her child from her own husband? Alice was tough, but still...

Now, with Jason, life had pillars, and Jenna felt secure. In her heart, she wished Jason was more of a poet. But she wouldn't exchange the prosaic for originality for anything. Was she giving something up of herself, she wondered fleetingly? And what about Alice? she could be irascible and infinitely sad. Would she ever make peace with this new family, and did she even think of it as one? These were the things that haunted Jenna, who felt a slight fissure in her own core. Alice was the person she loved most in the world. That was the simple truth.

She sat next to her daughter on the bed, and they both listened to Jason's story of his own tonsillectomy when he was five—how the shot felt like a wasp's sting, and the next thing he knew he was crying for water and his mother. He never ate so much ice cream in his life. Best of all, someone brought him a mysterious gift, which made him nervous at first, as it had a face that could change a thousand ways. But once at play, he became absorbed in all the possible traits that could transform his new friend, and he played with him for hours, for days, losing the face to a protruding pair of glasses, watching it disappear behind a beard, finding it again, his old freckled friend, then teasing it with an earring, and laughing as the face retaliated with a stuck-out tongue. Alice and Jenna looked on with surprising delight as Jason became that five-year-old right before their eyes. It made him seem more real to Alice, who sat beside him all evening as he read the paper and she watched some junk on TV.

After three days, Rodger called. Alice was alone and could no longer stand the ache of waiting that loomed over everything she did. She knew that it was Rodger when she heard the ring and rushed into her room and shut the door, despite the empty house. She answered breathlessly, mad at herself for showing how much it meant to her. As if the way one breathed could make it all right again. Awkwardly he asked how she was feeling, and Alice didn't know quite what to say. "I'm okay," she replied with a faint quiver in her voice and hated him for asking such a stupid question. Was this actually Rodger? She couldn't recognize him at this distance; he was so far away. For a person who prided himself on fixing things... well, this was shattering. She felt nauseated by the imminent break-up and hoped she wouldn't puke. In the long pause that followed, Alice had time enough to take a breath and pull herself together; her racing heart braced her somewhat, although it made her dizzy. She could no longer stand the apprehension, so let the ax fall as it may. At least it would have fallen, so be done with it.

"Listen, Alice..." Rodger felt like a lout and didn't recognize himself as someone who caused pain. He felt a visceral twinge as he became this person but simply didn't know what else to do. He couldn't continue living with this odd feeling he had when he was with Alice, and even when he wasn't. It felt like he was outside the experience and couldn't get back in. In truth, this odd watching feeling seemed to permeate most things about him, like his job, his family. It had to mean something. As it became more acute, he felt he couldn't stand it and just had to flee, from her, from everything.

"Here it comes," she thought stiffly. Unable to sense his anguish, she cut him off. "Rodger, don't. I know it's over. But can I at least see you to talk about it?" She would go out with a fight after all; and yet the fighter was infinitely sad. "I mean when I'm feeling better. My throat is absolutely *killing* me," she added, with a lightness that he had to know was fake.

He remained outside. But if he'd let himself visualize her from his end of the line, he might've felt the sadness too. "Maybe in a while. I think we both need some time," he was quick to reply, aware of how banal it sounded after all they had been through over those years and their deep connection. "I *am* sorry," he added, echoing his thought, repelled to find that he sounded all the more trite when what he felt was actually remorse. Alice was bewildered, confused, yearned for it to reverse itself that very second, but terrified of an explanation that would leave her scalded.

"Okay... goodbye," she said quickly, coming to her own defense, then heard his voice trail off. He was saying something she couldn't hear; what could it have been? Then the line went dead. "Coward!" she said out loud and felt a surge of contempt for this man whom she still loved. Even kids are braver! And her thoughts turned to little Adam.

II. Adam

"In history," Adam said one Sunday morning, "it seems like vaginas weren't very popular."

"What makes you say *that*?" Emma laughed, turning towards him, then saw how serious he looked. She wondered what had prompted such a remark. It wasn't the content that startled her—her child spoke freely about things that crossed his mind—but the fact of it breaking the silence of a long hour. She glanced down at the *Encyclopedia of Mythology* before him on the table, lying open to Titian's *Diana and Actaeon*, featuring the bathing goddess with a lavender cloth draped modestly over her upper thighs.

"Breasts were popular, and so were penises. But not vaginas. Why is that?"

He wasn't sure which was stranger, the way the women in the paintings were all covered up, or this halted conversation. Why did Mama look like that all of a sudden? Was something wrong? He eyed her intently and then repeated his question, wanting her to explain and to look happy again.

It was all in the details: this drapery aestheticized fear, awe and repression—centuries-old—of so much that is female, Emma mused, the thoughts quickly broken by her insistent son. She returned to the task, not knowing where to start to answer him in any serious way and wondering how to put it for a six-year-old. Besides, Adam's recent sense of justice was something to be reckoned with. "That's not fair! We are going to undress everybody and paint them all," she imagined him replying, indignant.

Raising a child was no simple matter and, like most, Emma made it up as she went along—but, unlike most, had not pretended, and would not pretend, to have the confidence that others displayed. Her ways of knowing were more sensory. It was not that she lacked intellect; she could lose herself for hours in analytical reflection. But when it came to assuredness, one could find it in the way she gripped rocks and branches on a steep hike, or how she could reveal the essence of an object in a drawing, or how she could become one with the rain when she ran across a soaking lawn. So motherhood was not a thing she took for granted, ever, and doubted it was even a universal condition. Every day brought with it different demands, challenging her to figure things out as best she could.

She looked on at her son, a quizzical fellow, who pondered all that was strange or mean in the world—anything at all, in fact, that he didn't understand. She considered Luke's recent comment about him being quite a sturdy little guy, unafraid to stand up and speak his mind. Emma, too, felt outraged by the world's injustices and recognized the pinkness in Adam's face when he got mad, the flush that easily rose and stung his cheeks. She wanted to come to his rescue but fell silent in frustrated embarrassment, which made for an imperfect harmony between them. Of course, she didn't want to worry him: on the contrary. She wanted to inform yet comfort. But what to do about reality and the more disturbing ways of the world? She could, after all, ponder Adam's question till she came up with the best possible answer, and at times she certainly would entertain a question, turning it over and over, but today she had other preoccupations, that had to do with trees, bark, dirt, and roots.

From Adam's point of view, his parents didn't always see what really mattered. First and foremost, they didn't appreciate his deep need to fool around, which, for him, was not at all trivial. He saw it in his father's eyes when it was time for bed, and he could anticipate the scolding for his silliness. If you couldn't fool around, what was the point of anything? Seeing for himself how harsh the world could be, it was all the more important to get in as much fun as possible.

Some days he felt himself pulled between wanting to go out and play and wanting to stay in the quiet safety of his room, nervous about discovering something out there that might scare him. Luckily, his parents thought that outside and inside were equally okay. They liked to be in *their* rooms, Mama in her studio and Daddy at his desk. Mama did love trees and parks, though, and would often whisk him away with her and, just when they would go back home, Daddy would be in the mood to play catch outside. Sometimes he didn't have a choice. Actually, he often didn't, come to think of it.

He didn't mind so terribly much; he liked being with them despite the inevitable fight about the objects he wanted to bring home. Couldn't they see these things had feelings? How could they leave a soda can all alone in the gutter? Once in a while would come the great concession; Mama or Daddy would even encourage him to bring home something he'd found out there, and what a lucky break *that* was! Adam's most special memory was of a bottle cap he was kicking home for over a mile at least, with his Mama by his side. It was a Coke cap, nice and red and very kickable; not many of those around, Mama said: a real treasure! Well, he was having such a good time, just kicking it all the way home, when all of a sudden it bounced through a steel grid in the sidewalk, landing in a pit a good eight feet below. He was stunned by the sudden loss. Mama called Daddy and, what felt like seconds later, through a veil of tears, he saw his father come into focus, striding towards them. What was it he was waving in his hand? A magnet! A magnet tied to a string! Let the street be dirty! Daddy laid all the way down on it, his cheek resting on the sidewalk, and slowly lowered the magnet into the depths of the pit. Adam's heart raced with the memory of the Coke cap jumping up and sticking to the magnet. Luke slowly pulled it up as Adam's heart was racing with suspense: would it fall back down, forever this time? It wasn't until it was tucked into his hand that he could breathe a sigh of relief, and he heard himself sigh just like that now, comforting his friend all the way home, turning it over and over in his palm until he laid it safely on his bedside table, where it remained ever since.

Adam glanced back at the Titian with growing impatience, and just as Emma was about to offer a short sociological explanation of the woman's body as object, he blurted out: "Did they ever paint *you*, Mama?"

"No, they didn't." It was likely Adam was referring to the Renaissance artists in his book: long ago could easily become yesterday in his world, so his mother might well be the subject of a sixteenth-century painting. When did a person enter sequential history, Emma wondered. And at what age would Adam distinguish his imaginings from real possibility? She wasn't sure she always lived by such distinctions herself. She remembered seeing him the other day in the hallway, announcing to no one in particular that he was going to destroy gravity. With his arms out and crooked, he seemed to be flying. He must've felt, at that moment, that he actually *was* flying.

Emma did remember imaginings of her own that would co-mingle with the laws of physics. For the most part, she could content herself with dreams. As a child she cherished the sensation of flight, which took on the form of gliding in her teenage years. The sensation of the lift would remain for days, a secret in her body. Once she'd grown up, the dream recurred more sporadically, and the flight, then the glide, mutated into floating as if attenuated by adulthood. They weren't so bad, actually, these new terms dictated by her psyche: She would find herself in some unknown room at a cocktail party, wandering about, talking to people here, then there, when, for no apparent reason, she would jump lightly, and rise, and then hover, some six or seven feet off the floor. The gentleness of the feeling made it somehow more real even than flying. It was *really happening*, she'd marvel—then wake up confused and disappointed. Later, after Adam was born, the flying and floating ceased altogether. Motherhood seemed to pull her down to earth where her child needed her, his own dream flights taking him to scary places. From time to time, he'd cry out for her, his whole body filled with terror and the intolerable loneliness of waking up all by himself.

"They haven't painted you because they haven't *seen* you," he continued, afraid he might have hurt her feelings. She was truly the best mom in the world, except when she got mad, and then her face would get hard, and she would go to some faraway place. His mother had a fiery soul, and her reactions were intense. When she didn't seem present, Adam would get nervous. Solid as he was, he had a fear of loss that pinned itself on things that Emma would never have guessed could anguish him. But then, a moment later, he'd turn his attention elsewhere—for instance, to one of the super-hero stories that he devised for his "public", the mysterious audience awaiting his next movie: *Spare Tire*, about a girl who rolled herself into a wheel and rolled out of reach of a villain coming after her. "But it costs a hundred dollars to produce, and I don't have enough money!" he complained bitterly to her one day.

"They'll just have to wait until you can afford it," she had told him. Well, he was glad about how changeable moods could be, always glad when she would come back to him.

As he closed his book, Adam remembered that he would have to go to school the next day and got a lump in his throat. "Do I *have* to go?" he asked for the hundredth time that year. Emma tried to distract him by showing him a different painting, but he was clearly done for the moment. It was spring, and it was still hard for him to go to kindergarten, and the thought of it took over everything for both of them. Emma worried endlessly even though she knew that he was fine after the teary goodbye.

"Don't worry, Adam. Thinking about it is way worse than being there," she told him, remembering the mysterious sadness that overcame her at 8:45 each morning.

Emma jumped with the sudden interruption of her thoughts by Adam's furious foot giving a sudden blow to the table leg. "*It's not fair!*" he yelled. Why did he *have* to do *anything*?

He ran into his room, where he cried for a moment into a stuffed giraffe, then found some solace looking around at his books, action figures, animals of every shape and size, boxes brimming with pencils, crayons, markers, and all his pads filled with drawings of gods and centaurs, Batman and Wonder Woman, the Beatles, stickers, and spiders. His growing rock, acorn and leaf collection smelled a bit earthy in one corner of the room, but he wouldn't let anyone near it, afraid that a grown-up would do something irrational, like sort it, or worse.

He was good and tired of school but had a sinking feeling that he would have to go, and, drawing a breath to steady himself, he went back into the living room, demanding to look at his nature magazine. He burrowed a comfortable place on the couch amid the pillows and communed with a pair of beavers hard at work on their lodge. How he would've loved to join them! The carefully lain sticks and branches made such a perfect little house! When the lodge was finished, he'd swim underwater and watch them make their dens from below. He'd mount the guard for hours, the mud paint on his face, daring any creature or human to approach. Cute little beavers! The kits spent practically all their time playing!

Emma finally managed to get him out of the house for a trip to Central Park, and the two set off without Luke, who practically never joined them on these expeditions. He was too engrossed in his work, content to stay behind and watch the sparks of untamed thoughts whirl around. That was the part he liked best, the proliferation of ideas, the sequence without narrative, bits of dialogue without apparent context. After some days of these kinds of irruptions, a concept would begin to form, and then it was all he could think about, and he'd work on it day and night for weeks, months, sometimes years, hoping it would make it to the stage, despite the odds. If there was one place Luke *hated*, it was Broadway, with those musical concoctions that usurped the imagination with incessant spectacle, leaving viewers no space to dream, in performance spaces with names like American Airlines Theater. In protest, he wrote a stark drama, not devoid of humor, that pitted an innocent man against a culture that sought to rob him of all reverie. "Move along!" the world said, as the dreamer stopped to examine a lamppost, or the colorful peak of the Empire State Building, or ask a stranger what they were thinking of, or if they were poor or sad. Mason, the protagonist, lived this way and had amazing adventures. But at a price. While he beckoned the audience to join him, he remained apart, a freak. At least that's what a critic in the *Times* wrote about the character on opening night. While Moorhead found the play "innovative and poetic" (Luke wanted to puke when he read that line), he called the motive "irrational and childish." Every time she went to see the show, Emma wept at the end. It wasn't the culture that made her cry. It was the loneliness that filled the silence when the final curtain fell. Was Luke so lonely? In their house, they all made claims to solitude; she thought it was all their riches...

It was a long shot, but Playtime, the gutsy little theater on East 4th, took a chance on it, and *Dreamer* played to a

packed house for six weeks and, by popular demand, continued for a full year. "One of the best writers to come along in
decades," wrote Ralph Peterson, a different critic altogether,
who became Luke's steady lunch companion at The Canteen,
where they would talk through their ideas and the books
they'd read. Luke was at work on his next drama, *Skyline*,
about the New Poor in America; he was researching the
shelter system in NYC when Emma called out that they were
leaving for the Park.

"Okay," he yelled distractedly, sorry moments later, missing the sound of Adam's chatter that somehow encouraged
him to go on with his work. Not that it was so bad lately,
now that he was finally getting some attention, and things
actually seemed possible. With his advance, he wouldn't have
to take one of those boring translation or writing jobs, not
for a year anyway, if his calculations were correct. But they
barely paid the bills as it was, even with the advance. They
had so many expenses: for example, this new babysitter
would cost something. He paused to ponder this mysterious
Alice, a student of Emma's, who would watch Adam some
afternoons. He felt vaguely tense as if her presence had
already filled the air. Would he be able to relax or, more
importantly, work—with a stranger in the house? They were
so private... and this whole idea of paying someone to watch
Adam was foreign to his sensibility. It was all very absorbing,
this newcomer, and Luke tried out different personalities on
the girl, undecided what kind of relationship he would have
with her. Paternal? Fraternal? Employer? They all made him
cringe, and he fell into a distracted discomfort. Well, there
was no way around it. If they were to get any work done that
summer, they would have to get help. And he became hopeful again, swatting the irritation from his mind, promising
himself that he wouldn't dwell on it, this advance being such
a gift. He would finish that play if it killed him. In a flight of

fancy, he thought he might play the main character himself and dove back into his work.

The path down to the boat basin fascinated Adam, who filled his bulging pockets with as many rocks and leaves as he could fit, then pointed his fistfuls of ever more treasures towards his mother so she could hold them while he stooped to pick up the next wonderful thing that he had to take home—a piece of colored cellophane! How did it get there? It shone red on the cement path, surprisingly. Weren't shadows always grey or black? Mama said something about *opaque* objects and how the sun couldn't see through them, unlike cellophane, which was *transparent*. Adam imagined the sun going around, peering here and there into objects, and decided that his mother made this up. If only she'd just admit it was magic! But he was having some doubts: in school the other day, when Adam showed up without his front tooth, he told the kids that the tooth fairy had left him a silver dollar.

"There's no such thing as the tooth fairy," Georgette retorted. "It's your mother!" Now Georgette was his good friend, and she seemed so sure of herself, as she looked at him with her gentle eyes that glistened despite her strong voice, and she had this flowing light brown hair and a half-smile most of the time. Adam completely trusted her; they had been inseparable since nursery school. He worried the whole rest of the day, not wanting to believe her but suspecting that she might be right. Did that mean there was no such thing as magic *at all*? No such thing as *powers*? He clutched the utility belt that he always wore to Central Park. Well, *he* believed, remembering Peter Pan when he yelled out, "Clap if you believe in fairies!" when poor Tinker Bell was dying. Adam clapped his hands until they hurt, and that was why she came back to life, because he and other children believed in her, so there had to be magic and fairies and heroes after all!

He was squatting, immersed in the red shadow, and would've stayed there, waving his hand over, and then under, then alongside the cellophane, experimenting with the light, pondering this thing called *transparent* when his mother gently reminded him that they were on a mission. He thrust the piece of cellophane toward her, explaining it would be the leaves of the tree sculpture Mama promised they would make out on the balcony. Would those red leaves make red shadows everywhere? And what would happen to the tree in the wind and the rain? Would it fall over? Not if they made it very strong, as much like a tree as possible, with roots even, and that solid branch over there was just the thing. He dragged it back to Emma with a probing smile.

"Oh, no, Adam, we can't possibly take *that* home!" Her hands were full, and her face was closed to the idea, but he just had to have it, and she would have to carry it, since it was as tall as he was, and how could he run around and find more twigs and stuff if he had to hold it? So, he leaned the branch against her leg and ran off before she could lay down the law, which she wouldn't, remembering a piece of plywood in a dumpster that turned into a totem pole. He didn't know what *totem* meant but imagined it was an Indian dog that would protect them if only he would do a good job transforming that ordinary piece of wood into a colorful story. About ten totem poles leaned on walls throughout the house. His very favorite showed a mermaid reaching up out of the sea to seize the sun and bring it back down to the depths. This was where the sun went at night when it got dark, he explained, having watched it set over the ocean in Maine, dipping out of view at nightfall. He was horrified when Mama asked if the ball of fire would sizzle when it touched the sea, and quickly set her straight about the secret world of water, where nothing died, and creatures of all kinds could breathe without air. Besides, didn't she realize that the sun came back up every morning? What was wrong with her? He hoped this new Alice wouldn't ask him such ridiculous questions. Well, Mama did seem to know about lots of things, especially totem poles and markers and googly eyes.

Hey! Maybe he could make a *looking tree* by putting googly eyes on all the leaves and the trunk of the sculpture! But what was she doing now? He wandered over to her, planted near an elm, his treasures piled nearby, as she looked intently at the bark that she was drawing in her sketchpad, wondering how she could reproduce the very thing that she was seeing. Considering it a moment, he realized the drawing was remarkably different, for all that the grooves and curves and texture looked the same. There was a feeling about it that he couldn't explain even though it was black and white and grey. All of her drawings were, which made him wonder if she could even see colors, remembering her inability to explain the red shadow on the path. But even if she *could* see colors, why did everything have to be pencil shadows? He raced around the tree in an effort to distract her from the drawing.

"But aren't we going to the statue?" Alice in Wonderland was always their final destination in the Park, so why was she taking so long? "Mama, come on!"

Emma gathered her things regretfully. It was quite a fine trunk, and she tried to think of when she might come back to finish sketching its bark and how to find that elm again amid all the others on that gently rolling hill. "Okay! I'm coming!" She followed Adam as he raced down past the boat basin without glancing at the sailboats, which never seemed to interest him. He did love to feed the birds, but there was no time for that! Eagerly he looked to see if anyone was climbing on the statue and pictured the maneuvers he would have to make into Alice's lap where he would stay for hours if Mama let him.

"Here we go again," thought Emma with a sigh. Adam could engage in a conversation so elaborate that she gave up months ago following his "dialogue" with Alice and her friends.

Adam also liked Alice's cute little kitten—not the Cheshire, who was a little scary—and would pet its head and play with its paws. Other kids would clamber up to have their picture taken, and he would play with them, but they could never stay long, their parents ordering them down as soon as they had shut the video or snapped the photo, sometimes grousing that they couldn't get the shot they wanted. But no amount of coaxing could get Adam to share Alice's lap with anybody else, and Emma didn't get involved because the statue was for playing, not for posing.

As she watched him in animated conversation with the Mad Hatter, Emma recalled her talk with the other Alice about looking after Adam. It was the end of the semester, and she had to plan for the summer and the long hours when Adam wasn't off in science camp and into the fall thereafter. Alice would be interested, she hoped, because the girl seemed genuinely nice even though they'd barely spoken over the course of the semester. At one point, Alice had asked her to look at a pastel she had done of a Hudson Valley landscape—a view from the high cliffs in the tradition of the painters before her. But this was different. The River curved serenely through those 19th-century paintings while the real drama was in the rising cliffs and sky. Kensett, Emma's favorite, was in a class by himself; his study of rock formations along the River's edge in *The Old Pine* was compelling in its proximity to the depths without plunging there. The windblown pine craned out from the cliff into the sky in harmonious solitude; but Emma's eye was all on the shoreline stones, their molding grey cut through with reddish veins and their exquisite meeting with the water in deep reddened shadows.

Here she remained, sea level, for hours, in the detail of those rock shadows. Of course, all the paintings of the Falls, or any waterfall, from that School of River painters were alive with the rushing water. But, in general, the Hudson was a wide, still stream, at the base of a hike into sublime serenity.

Alice's pastel was reminiscent of those scenes, if only, perhaps, in geographical view. Was this Breakneck Ridge? Emma beheld the River where something more darkly mysterious and erotic erupted in the nightly hour of the landscape, harking back somewhat to Albert Pinkham Ryder and the way personal perception becomes the source of illumination. In Alice's pastel, the light source came from below, inhabiting the River rather than from the moon, a suggested smudge in the sky. The force of the River in the silent solitude was almost disturbing to Emma, who found herself peering ever deeper into the blue and black currents until she had to look away. Alice was quite brave to venture there. Emma's work searched for something else in the things of nature. She didn't think she had ever attempted a landscape and was not drawn to the sweep of the world. Lately, though, she felt a growing fascination with roots and dirt. But in general, her pull was to the still life and the subtle inner life of, say, a vegetable. Her series of peppers was well known in certain circles. Jake Stein liked them, and that was all that really mattered.

His work was astonishing, catching the point of awakening. Such things he could do with clouds and birds! She happened on one drawing in a gallery on 26th Street—fireflies darting about, and yet suspended, glowing; alive, yet fading in the dusk; mortality in the sky. She got up the courage to approach him as he was leaving Cooper Union one day, she herself coming home from a class on Stuyvesant Street. She had a small portfolio with her and asked if he would take a look. They lost themselves in hours of conversation, grabbing coffee at the Mud Truck, which electrified the afternoon with visceral longing as music by the Doors poured into the plaza. Every homeless person in the neighborhood was stopping by, it seemed, to score a cookie or a drink from those nice Mud Truck kids.

There was this whole alternative economy at Astor Place, with endless bartering of books, CDs, espressos, metro rides, punk boots. These prized possessions stretched themselves out like an urban picnic in the shade of the earth-colored Cooper Union, the great brownstone with arching windows from the 19th century. Just around the corner, at number 41, the school's new building provided a playful counterpoint to the original. In fact, it looked like a 3-D pencil drawing, with cups of light pouring in through the roof. Emma held on to these buildings as if her life depended on it, terrified of the cold, canned real estate that was plowing its way through the city, destroying the heart and soul of Manhattan's neighborhoods.

Emma loved Astor Place and would meet Jake there to show him her latest turnip or bunch of bananas. She wasn't quite as good at drawing fruit. Jake suggested that she open it up—not slice it neatly, but break it open to reveal the coconut's jagged meat or the grapefruit's bulging pulp. Well, he was definitely onto something because it was the monotony of the skin that bothered her. Peppers were smooth, but they had all those folds and came in weird shapes—nothing like an apple, which just sat there, placid. One day she came across a magnifying glass in Luke's study, and then felt differently about how imperfect and porous grapefruit skin could actually be. She realized she could forget about the pulp altogether and spent months on a series of peel drawings—apples, grapefruit, oranges—but each time had to work fast before they started coloring and shriveling, then rotting, as the hours wore on. She shrank from the morbid allure, until she finally got brave and could sit with a thing decomposing. She filled pads with shriveling skins of rotting orange peels.

Vegetables were next, and she thought she might attempt a potato but decided that there would be little there; she could imagine the peels lying sadly on newspaper like flat, mushy coins. Between a peeled potato skin and a whole dusty, bumpy potato bulging with eyes, there was no contest. Then again, she could always let the entire potato rot. Now that would be something good.

If anyone were to ask what she thought about, what would she say? *Fruit* or *vegetables, pulp and skin, tree bark* or *roots*. It didn't make for very good conversation, did it, and wasn't much help to the world. She felt obsessed, really. She *had* to draw, and she had to draw *these* things, and preferred not to ask why, but worried that it was a strange way to spend a life. She heard Adam calling her, and her thoughts swerved back to Alice and her enthusiasm about babysitting for Adam. With her around, she might get in a few hours a day. She was pretty sleep-deprived working only at night.

She saw him pointing to the crocodile beneath the statue, and away he crawled under the giant mushroom, listening for the clock that always made Hook panic and yelp. Adam gradually got lonely for his father and asked to talk to him. Emma dialed home, he grabbed the phone, and curled up against his ticking friend and carried on a conversation with Luke. As usual, this went on forever until Emma got antsy. She gathered up the branch, the cellophane, the acorns and the sticks, the rocks and leaves, and struggled over to the subway, with Adam trailing behind, still talking to his father.

"Mama!" Adam screamed. "I'm scared!" It was just moments after Emma left his room that night. She thought he was fast asleep and was all ready to crawl into bed with *The Rainbow*.

Luke wasn't coming home until much later, so she was on her own. All evening Adam had been unusually quiet and looked shaken when he went to bed.

"What's the matter, honey?" she asked softly, making her way back toward his bed.

"It's not true about apes, is it?"

It was something from their conversation of the day before when Luke's friends had come for lunch. "How did people get here?" Adam asked them all, and she told him about evolution. She thought he'd find it interesting, but she should have known better. But what was wrong with telling Adam about evolution? He wasn't a creationist! Or was he? "I find that *very unusual*," Adam said indignantly. "I don't think it happened that way at all. If it did, apes and people would be changing right now. Do you see any apes changing into people? I don't! I think people are born *whole*, from the earth mother, Hera." He quickly left the table and went to listen to some music on the far side of the room. She hadn't given it another thought.

Realizing how affected he really was by the conversation, she tried to put it all into context as he sat up tensely, awaiting her response.

"It's not the kind of change that anyone can see. It takes millions of years."

This only scared him more.

"But people are *not* changing into apes, right, Mama?" He burrowed into her shoulder.

"Adam, a person can't change into an ape or any other kind of animal. It just can't happen. The only thing that changes a person is age. We get older." He looked up at her, considering this idea. Mama was right about getting older. His six years made him feel a little different, and when his front tooth fell out, it sure made him *look* different. But there were other things that were troubling him. They read a story in school about a selfish boy who turned into a pig. That was awful! All day he waited for the moment when he could burst into Daddy's room to ask if it was true. Daddy told him about *exaggerations* and how they helped you understand how bad or good something was. Well, no one needed to exaggerate to *him* by turning children into pigs! He did feel better, though, talking with Daddy, who always had good words that would put a name to something. Adam repeated back *exaggeration* in an effort to push the story from his mind.

"I'm still scared, Mama." His voice was trembling.

"Don't worry. I'm going to sit right here with you and protect you." At this, Adam imagined her fighting off a hideous witch and fell silent.

"Tell me what you're afraid of."

"I'm afraid of being changed into something or that you'll change into something!" Didn't she see? Mama had a good way of telling him how plants grew, but when she started in with *evolution*, or why he had to go to school, it was too much. Still, there was no one in the world who could cuddle with him like Mama, even though she made him mad sometimes.

Emma propped up a pillow and lay back on it with her arm around him. She sang him song after song, her voice working better than any of her reassurances, and he made her sing *She's got a ticket to ride* for a good hour. Finally, the three hundredth repetition of "My baby don't care" made him forget about apes, and pigs, and people changing, and his chest began to rise and fall in the breathful rhythm of sleep.

Back at her worktable, Emma studied the sweet potatoes sitting stupidly on the cutting board. She sat there for a few minutes, then became irritated. Maybe the problem was the cutting board; its hard flatness and symmetry couldn't hold the bulbous, warty potatoes. She replaced it with a faded, green-striped kitchen towel. That made them more sympathetic, huddling there on the cloth. She laid a paring knife beside them, but the imminent drama was too threatening, so she quickly hid the weapon in the kitchen drawer. She turned toward the table and, sensing the potatoes were now more contained, focused on their unusual shape and dusty skin and started sketching.

It was strange having all these feelings for potatoes—or rather, feelings for potatoes that, as she worked them out on paper, started taking on a whole different kind of life. Well, not *entirely* different, like an ape turning into a person... poor Adam. What was that about? Suddenly her eyes were stinging. It all felt lonely in the room, as if devoid of shadows, the kind that hovered and surrounded things and held them.

She remembered something her mother told her one gray morning. It must have been some April. The crocuses were poking up out of the ground through the melting snow; as a child she'd loved that moment more than anything. She could still feel herself at dawn, in her blue and white bathrobe with chickens on it, flying down the stairs and leaping out into the garden to be first to spot the crocuses, then panting back up the stairs to tell Daddy that the flowers were coming up. Groggy, he would take her hand, and they would go down to the garden where he'd peer into the flower bed with Emma breathless by his side, pointing at the earliest flower in the whole world.

But on that later April morning, Emma didn't run out to the crocuses but merely gazed at them from the porch window, not because she was grown up, but because it was the day of Grandma's funeral, and the room, and the world, felt empty. She had had a premonition—a dream of Grandma calling to her in a frightened voice. "Oh, she's completely fine!" Emma's mother said abruptly when she tried to tell her about it. But one month later, Grandma was diagnosed with stage 4 cancer and spent her final weeks in a coma. When Emma went to see her in the hospital, her grandmother's hand grasped her own, despite the sleep from which she would never wake. That morning, after the burial, Emma's mother was sitting at the kitchen table, very quiet, very still. Then, suddenly, she said: "We are all alone." Emma filled with panic, like a child, like an orphan. That's what it must be like, she realized. This is mourning... then she put it out of her mind, not wanting to ponder it further. Thinking about it now, she figured that her mother might have felt some kind of loneliness her whole life; Grandma's death had only forced her to face it. Emma felt an inner reflex of rebellion; she did not feel that implicit loneliness, at least not often, and wondered what it was like for Adam.

She got up to look in on him. His peaceful face, lit dimly by a three-quarter moon, was so beautiful that she wondered why she'd never done his portrait. But when she tried to picture it—his exhausted slumber translated into a haze of charcoal and smudged white pencil—it seemed wrong. How could she capture the mood of fear and then relief from fear? And, somehow, it felt like a betrayal. Drawing him, when he didn't know it, while he was asleep? She didn't have it in her. She went back to her sweet potatoes.

At 6:45, the doorman buzzed. "Alice is here to see you."

Emma's heart skipped a beat. In his light blue pajamas, smelling sweetly of his bath, Adam stood by, his whole body

filled with anticipation. She opened the door to her smiling student.

"He's *so* ado*r*able!" Adam jumped with pleasure, and the party began. Emma watched them run off to play and tried to recall the last time she felt such joy herself. There was the kind that gripped her when she gazed at a tree in winter, when the crooked branches rose out bare against the dim white sky and a hole in the trunk, knotted around the edges, dipped into the depths of the tree; or when Luke was content with his writing, which was rare, as his creations were the stuff of smoldering, wrought finally into a readable thing; or when she and Adam made up some impossibly silly game. But her joy had a different resonance from theirs; it was more acute, almost painful. And it felt timeless for only so long. More often than not, it was accompanied by the awareness of it. Adam and Alice had no consciousness of their delight, thrust as they were in the pure spontaneity of their meeting and existing simply as they were. Although Alice was pretty much an adult, she still had this riotous mermaid within her.

Adam was busy showing Alice his toys. A half-hour later, when Emma peeked in, they were immersed in a game involving animals with secret powers that revealed themselves only at night. She watched unobserved how he entered other worlds with a deer imbued with flight, sailing out of his hand across the forest sky. She knew what this was like, and it was the very thing she loved the most about drawing—immersion to the point of forgetting everything else, her consciousness somehow withheld, except for the thing before her, so she would actually jump when someone called her name. It was the closest she came to floating again. Emma left them to it.

Content with his new friend, Adam thought he would initiate Alice into his favorite game, which began atop the bunk bed in the company of Dad, who had devised with him the master plot: the transformation of merpeople into humans. The true interest of the game, however, had to do with arguing, and as far as Adam was concerned, there was nothing more gratifying than to watch King Triton go at it with Ariel. As the story went, the king wouldn't let his daughter go on dry land because he thought humans were barbarians and wanted to protect her from them. Ariel would use all her rhetorical skill to convince her father to *see for himself* that *not all* humans were barbarians. Adam would direct his father, who played both merfather and daughter, and he would grin from ear to ear when Ariel, triumphant, would magically turn their tails into legs. They would then walk onto the surface of the human world where, after some adventures in a small beach town, Triton would fall in love with a beautiful, albeit legged woman and try to get her to go back with him to live under the sea. She would inevitably resist for the simple reason that merpeople ate only seaweed, and it would surely make her sick. In the heat of the moment, Jafar and Alladin would make an appearance, and connive to accomplish their own ends, Jafar to rule the world under the sea, and Alladin to win Ariel's hand. These sub-plots were introduced with great enthusiasm, as they would lend themselves to further arguing, and it would all go on for hours or until Dad fell asleep.

Alice, who had a mind of her own, departed from the script with her own rebellious behavior. She had Ariel go on dry land even though Triton had forbidden it. This was radical for Adam, who was eager to learn the outcome of such defiance: Would Triton punish Ariel for disobeying him? Would she then have to choose between life on land or down in the sea? Such a terrible choice! The things kids have to go through! Would Ariel even be able to live without her father? Or would Triton understand how much it meant to Ariel to leave the sea and forgive her? Would he follow her onto dry land to protect her? Just when the mergirl was about to meet a human for the first time, Emma reminded them that it was time for Alice to leave.

"No, Mama! I have to find out the end of the story!"

He was soon comforted by Alice's assurance that next time they would pick up right where they left off, and Emma told him Alice would be with him every other day that summer, and even before that, meeting him at the bus stop, in fact, and spending two or three days a week until the end of school. Satisfied, he ran off to his father's room, ready to astonish him with this plot twist of the disobedient daughter. Knowing Dad, he would gladly explore this idea the next time they were up on the bunk. But then, he thought he might just want to keep on playing the game with Alice and wondered if he should feel bad about it. Would Daddy mind? And, come to think of it, where *was* Daddy that whole time? He hadn't come out to meet Alice, which Adam demanded on the spot. The child, who already felt that Alice was his special friend, made the introductions. The four of them fell silent for a moment, aware, perhaps, of some great change. Adam broke the silence, demanding that Luke watch a comedy with him, pulling him by the hand towards the TV in the back of the apartment.

Alice began to tell Emma about her tonsillectomy, which was scheduled for the upcoming week; she wouldn't be able to start until the end of May. A fearful look clouded Alice's face. Emma described her own tonsillectomy and how indignant she'd felt when they put her in a crib at *five*. She remembered waking up and screaming for water. She had to spend an extra night at the hospital after all the other children in her room had gone home, without ever being told why and wondering how her mother and father could possibly have let them keep her there. "Well," Alice said—not at all consoled by the story—"at least I won't have to sleep in a crib!" Everyone has a tonsillectomy story, Alice mused with a nervous smile. She didn't realize the operation loomed so large within the greater cultural memory. Must be the same for an appendectomy! She clutched her side, sweating, hoping she'd never have to go through one of those.

Adam and his dad were watching *Monkey Business*, and he was helpless with laughter. Emma described Adam's incurable love of comedy and how he had begged her for a pair of Groucho glasses and a mustache. He was utterly crushed when Georgette came over to play and dismissed Harpo, Chico, and Groucho, whom she had never heard of. Adam put on his disguise to act out a scene from *Duck Soup* and made several waddling turns around the room like Groucho, but all he got was a condescending smile. So he gave up but told her to go home and make her parents show her *Animal Crackers* or *A Day at the Races*, it didn't matter which. Could they still be friends, he asked Emma later that evening, if Georgette didn't like the Marx Brothers?

It wasn't that Adam didn't like a serious story, Emma thought to herself that night as she reflected on her conversation with Alice. It was the fact of stories themselves and their commanding presence in her child's life, which Alice had glimpsed during their first meeting. Emma remembered, back when he was barely walking, how his whole body would come alive when Luke read him *Green Eggs and Ham*. As much as he loved books from a very early age, he seemed to have his most intense narrative experience when he first saw *The Red Balloon*. Luke had given it to Adam as a Christmas present, forgetting how down and out Paris looked, the traces of German bombs haunting the urban landscape as children wandered about in a fatherless world, with no sense of security. Luke was struck that he had remembered only the film's charm, completely missing the contextual significance: a whole city was left to recover from the Occupation, and the devastating fate of the balloon was not a mere artifact of war's atrocity, but the persistence of aggression, and loss. As it happened, Adam was enthralled, insisting that they watch the movie with him a good twenty times that first week alone.

"The balloon understands, doesn't it, Mama?" He watched as it followed the lonely boy all over the city. "Love is *real!*" True, those boys trampled the red balloon, they were so mean, but Adam thought it would be good to stomp on things when you got mad. And in the end, that good boy got to fly up to the sky with all those other balloons that came to save him! How Adam wished he could be that boy! For the next six months, he collected helium balloons of every size and color so that his room always looked like a parade had just passed through it.

Back in the bedroom, Adam was marveling over Harpo and the way he dared to do the funniest things that shocked people, when it was really the case that there were so many rules just begging to be broken. Harpo walked on the table and stamped all the officer's foreheads at the checkpoint when asked to produce the passport that he didn't have. He threw all their official papers on the ground! He would cut in on the line with his brothers who would all try to pass as Maurice Chevalier, only Harpo, who didn't speak, hid a record player in his coat, and mouthed the famous "If a nightingale could sing like you." What a song to sing to those serious officers! Adam had a new hero.

"Why don't people act like that more often?" Adam asked his father wistfully, thinking over whether children could defy their parents or other grown-ups, like Ariel in Alice's story. Daddy liked it when he imitated Groucho, telling jokes and waddling around; but would he get mad if Adam ran around like Harpo did, pulling stunts like that and breaking all the rules? That kind of fooling around seemed to be in a whole different category. As much as he loved to go crazy, Adam didn't like to make his parents mad.

"People are often worried about what others think,"

Daddy told him, "and it makes them hold back from what they really want to do."

"Do you do what you really want?"

"Well, maybe not everything I want, but the most important things, like writing plays and being with you and Mommy."

"And what about the unimportant things, like Harpo's gags? Why aren't they just as good? Don't they count?"

"I don't know, Adam, I tend to think they're on another scale." Luke wasn't altogether content with that response. As insignificant as passing through a checkpoint might be, Harpo's gag brought to light how everyone accepted the policing of the world. He turned the question back to Adam.

"I'd like to walk on a table like Harpo when we're told to sit quietly and work," Adam replied, thinking how antsy he got on the red carpet at circle time, or in his seat when they had to sit still.

Luke's face registered alarm, though he inwardly smiled at his son's defiant energy.

"Don't worry, Daddy!" Adam laughed. "I'll think of something better!" Now it was the father's turn to be wistful. How could he encourage rebellion and protect his child from its harsh consequences at the same time? Not an easy line to walk, he thought.

Emma was surprised not to hear from Alice, who had promised to call after her operation. She dialed the number, worrying it wouldn't work out after all. She could hardly recognize her student's scratchy voice. Jenna called later that evening to explain that her daughter was going through a tough recovery from the tonsillectomy, complicated by a devastating breakup. She didn't think that Alice could start until sometime in June. She could come whenever she was ready, Emma told her without hesitation.

"Maybe a child's companionship would help," Emma suggested.

"I hope so," Jenna replied.

Emma swallowed an anxious thought.

III. Emma

She watched the young woman make her way down Bleecker Street toward Sixth Avenue—very punctual and dependable, Emma noted, as her student approached the stop where they'd planned to meet. There were two weeks left before the summer break, and Alice would quickly have to get used to this ritual where there was so much at stake. Were she to be but a minute late, all hell would break loose. It was lucky that Adam had taken such a strong liking to Alice and was eager to see her again.

Peering down city streets in search of the horizon was a reflex of Emma's, recurring many times a day ever since she'd moved to the city some ten years before. She had grown up in the smaller, more sprawling Lawrence, Kansas, whose hilly landscape knew no towers. Neighboring farmlands stretched out to the end of the sky in a patchwork of ocher, beige, green and brown crops. As a little girl, Emma rose at dawn, and would sit at her second-floor window perch, never, or hardly ever, missing the locomotive that appeared every morning at 6:20 a.m. way out in the distance, the mostly reddish-brown but also silver, blue and green cars rolling past the foot of the mountain range on the horizon until only its still, silent slopes remained in view. It was in her, this looking outwards, even, or especially, amid the steel, brick and stone of the city, looking outwards for the end of space, until she realized, recently, that she could cast her gaze more uninterruptedly (without buildings blocking her view) underground, into this new frontier that opened downwards in her drawings. Since Adam came into her life, looking out and down the hall or up the street took on a new protective connotation, as she watched over him, or searched for him, as he moved in and out of view. In general, she preferred to meet up with people outdoors, if you could call it that in NYC. Such gazing up and down streets created a slow and dramatic build-up to her encounters, and specifically to Alice's, who she was waiting for expectantly. Coming into view, the girl's countenance and bearing seemed somehow altered. This created a disruption in Emma's imaginings of this historic moment but not to the extent that it would impede on its significance: her student would now be the one to greet her son when the yellow bus pulled up. It was time.

That bus had almost ruined Adam's whole first month of kindergarten. The cool sweaty smell of the yellow machine, strange graffiti, the splintered glass window above one of the seats, and the inevitable pieces of sticky gum on the floor that jarred him, sensing sadness and anger. He didn't recognize the streets and felt overwhelmed and lost. Who knew where the bus might take him? Being told not to worry only made him worry more. He had happily gone places without Daddy and Mama before, to spend time with Charlie or Georgette. But for all that he liked adventure, taking the bus, every day, with kids he didn't know, was a real leap into the world, one that had vast implications. Not entirely sure if the bus was altogether a bad thing—the bus driver always smiled at him and some of the kids told funny stories—he decided he would deal with it by just not being ready. Despite what he thought a convincing argument that he was too young to take the bus, his parents thought otherwise, and he had no choice but to give in. This is what it meant to be in kindergarten, putting up with all kinds of things, like bossy kids telling him what kind of superhero he was allowed to be and learning how to write neatly. It occurred to him that the bus was something he might have some control over and once in a while would plead his youthful case again. Seeing the strain on her son, Emma would surprise him at dismissal from time to time and walk the way home with him, making up various games, which Adam preferred to the otherwise tense transition back home. Within a few months, however, she sensed a fundamental change and discovered it was the doing of a fifth-grader, Josh, who every day took Adam by the hand onto the rickety machine, sharing a seat and reassuring him that all was well. One day at the stop, Josh's mother confided that Josh had been scared of the bus, too, when he was little and felt sympathy for the younger child. In the end, it looked like Dad had been right all along, Adam told Emma that spring: if he had never taken the bus, he wouldn't have met Josh and the whole gang of other kids who got on with him. They made a little traveling family of their own, telling jokes and singing silly songs. And in the end, it was Emma, rather than Adam, who continued to struggle. The bus was always late, and she had trouble finding the blind confidence that rituals are made of, forever glancing down the avenue with the strain of fear until she saw the M35 roll into view. Adam would come tripping off with a triumphant smile.

As Alice came more distinctly into view, Emma noticed her sad eyes, slightly sunken, but which lit up with their old exuberance when they met her teacher's gaze. She had gotten awfully thin since Emma had last seen her; it had to be more than the tonsillectomy, Emma thought, struck by Alice's effort to look cheerful, and felt not so much relief as admiration for her student's courage. It was a historic event of sorts for Alice as well, walking back out into the world without Rodger, and she couldn't shake the feeling that she was hydroplaning. She hadn't noticed Emma till she was less than half a block from the bus stop, so focused was she on her feet as they made contact with the sidewalk, the gait intent on grounding itself. It would be so much easier in the park, Alice thought, imagining the soft springtime earth, and the thought lifted her spirits. The bustling of kids fresh out from various schools, and tourists gawking at the movie posters on Bleecker Street, was more stimulation than she'd had in weeks. In the quiet of her mother's New Jersey home, she continued alternately weaving and unraveling her idea of herself in relation to Rodger. On the eve of her departure, she could finally look out the window and be soothed somewhat by the clear skies. But now, back in the city, her anguish had returned, filling Alice with the uncertainty of what she would become, and if she even felt like becoming anything. But something pressed her forward, despite her low sick feeling and the constant lump in her throat, which, when Emma greeted her, Alice bravely swallowed, then blurted out a loud and clear, if ever so tentative, "Hi!"

Alice was surprised by her own excitement: that *was* her voice, wasn't it?—the voice of pleasure—which had been muted those past weeks, and her neck and shoulders relaxed at the sound. Grateful, she fixed her attention on Emma, who was pinning her gaze south down Sixth Avenue where the bus came suddenly barreling, so fast, Alice thought, that her heart skipped a beat as the orange engine screeched to a stop. Emma introduced her to the bus driver, who greeted her kindly. This was Adam's life, a whole world that she would soon get to know. She took his hand affectionately, and they embarked on their afternoon journey. Emma overheard Adam's immediate plea for ice cream. It had been just seconds for the new friends to take up exactly where they had left off: delighted. Already half a block ahead, Emma turned back to wave to the smiling pair, then raced off, her portfolio under her arm, to meet up with Jake, not altogether surprised by her own delight.

Alice and Adam couldn't run and tag the tree they'd picked out a block away, the destination of a spur-of-the-moment race—a walking-backward race, Adam suggested, with Alice wisely nixing it with the saner prospect of giant steps, face forward. They couldn't run, of course, with ice cream cones in their hands, it made no sense at all, said

Adam, who couldn't decide if he was more excited by the cone, the race, the visit to the Square, or being with his new friend again. It would be the first time in his life, but well worth the "*hey!*" Alice cried when, out of nowhere, and quite unpredictably, he chucked his half-eaten chocolate treat into the garbage and took off like a roadrunner down the sidewalk that would take him safely into the southwest entrance of the Square, laughing his head off at the sight of Alice gaining on him, her strawberry cone raised like a pink torch. With no time to lose, he made his way past the chess players, up and down over the giant molehills, deftly bounded over the bench from behind, crossed the path, quickly made his way over a second bench from the front, and smacked his hand against the old Silver Maple that sprung up majestically behind the Holley statue. Alice was by his side in seconds, her cone empty of the frozen red ball that had been scalped by a low branch. They made themselves at home at the foot of this tree, and basked in the cool shadow cast in a circle around them while Adam caught his breath and quieted his laughter, with Alice pretending to scold him, which only caused a fresh batch of giggles to well up, soon to subside in the afternoon heat.

They turned toward the tree and lay on their backs, arms bent and hands cupped under their heads and contemplated the great trunk that rose into its high canopy of notched leaves fluttering silver and green. They felt no need to talk at first, but soon mused aloud about the unusual pale bark, unlike the other trees in the park.

"It's white because a goodly witch has enchanted it," Adam explained.

"And it has golden streaks from the broth dripping down from her soup bowl in the sky," Alice returned.

Some remaining seeds detached themselves from the tree and spun down within catching distance from the two friends who swore to keep them forever. They remained near that tree for the rest of the afternoon, telling stories, playing hide and seek, and relaxing into silence until Alice jumped up, realizing it was 6:00, and grabbed Adam by the hand to run home, where Luke was stationed outside the door, ready to greet them the moment they stepped out of the elevator.

"*10 minutes late*," Alice said, embarrassed, but Luke waved it away, catching first and foremost the light that darted towards him from Adam's eyes.

"I miss Alice!" Adam blurted out incongruously as only seconds ago his mouth had been happily dripping with the best chocolate ice cream in the world—and which could only be found at Ben and Bill's in Bar Harbor, at least according to Adam, who had to duke it out with Emma who was partial to the Mt. Desert shop. It was a hot afternoon in July. They had just come down Kebo Mountain, an expedition along an obscure 19th-century trail and a secret to those who really knew Acadia. They had escaped to that national park every summer since Adam was born, but it was only now that he could climb the harder peaks and keep at it for miles, which was quite a feat for someone with such little legs. There was something about Adam's exhaustion that made Emma wince as she wiped his sad mouth, then remembered the climb up Gorham Mountain some years ago. Adam had just turned two at the time, and it was his very first hike. The parents set out with confidence but soon veered off mistakenly onto Cadillac Cliffs—neither had much sense of direction—and, as steep as it was, continued scaling the rocky terrain for another two miles until they found themselves gazing up, speechless, at a sharp incline.

"Better go up," the ranger who wandered over said, "to

get back on track. You'll quickly reach Gorham Mountain and an easy path back down." Emma slowly climbed the jagged boulders, clutching Adam tensely in her arms. His gaze never left the treetops as he looked back over her shoulder, and his breathing was a little shallow. Luke followed close behind, ready to catch them lest she slip. He thought he could hear her heart pounding. She dared not speak or look back or down. The top of the path, just 20 feet above them, felt miles away. To give herself courage, she pretended she was a sure-footed mountain goat with a newborn on its back, and there! She set Adam down at the top of the boulder path, the sweat pouring off her. As if on automatic, he tripped down the trail in a semi-conscious daze, his hand resting snugly in his father's grip. When they finally got home, they dove into a deep, long nap, with Emma waking first, all aches and pains, and in a fit of laughter, from the stress, no doubt. And now, this summer of Adam's 6th birthday, she considered how confidently he led the way up that same mountain the day before, stopping from time to time to pick up a magic wand, which Emma found weeks later back in the city, wrapped in a dish towel, hidden in the few remaining items of his suitcase that she finally had a moment to put away.

Emma looked at Adam's hands, then at her own, darkly stained from the wild blueberries that covered the peak of Kebo Mountain, like some small blue secret that multiplied before their eyes and that they shared with the deer and the increasingly random black bear. Adam had dashed into the low bushes, yelling back to her about the *hundreds* he found as she paused, not far off, bent over one lovely cluster, wondering if she might try a sketch right then and there, but quickly abandoned the idea in favor of blueberry jam and thoughts about where to find mason jars. "Off the peak and into the pot," she mused and imagined her purply confection transforming a dreary winter morning in the city when she would set a jar upon the table with Luke and Adam looking on, fighting over who would get the first spoonful. Meanwhile, Adam was munching his way through the harvest, with just a couple of berries at the bottom of his bucket like the cub in *Blueberries for Sal*, while Luke sat on a boulder not too far away, gazing down at the Atlantic that hit the shore below, awed by the watery world that glistened infinitely, until his mind wandered back to the City, and how sublime Acadia was, in painfully stark contrast. The sound of Emma's laughter snapped him out of it, and he walked over to the empty pail that she was pointing at in disbelief. Adam boldly stood before them, blue hands on hips, eyes twinkling: king of the mountain. The idyllic spell soon dissipated for Emma as she started the trek back down the trail, nostalgic for the very moment they were living in, conscious of painful tensions that ran in the depths, like hidden streams underfoot.

Adam, too, was nostalgic with thoughts that tugged him away, out of Acadia and into the city where Alice was waiting for him, and which Emma didn't miss at all. As she finished her mocha chip cone, she found she couldn't let go of the gentle vistas of Kebo, its quiet beauty and the scrubby oaks that block out the otherwise plunging view. She would scale the mountain again, alone, later that afternoon, to harvest another pailful of berries. Immersed as she was in the mountain that rose behind her son who stood before her, she pulled away from her reverie at the sounds of his sighs. Adam's dream space in Acadia usually consisted of magicians or fairies following him up the mountain trails or onto the Great Sand Beach, but it was inhabited now by a real person whom he had come to love. Time seemed irritatingly endless to Adam as he sat on the bench, protected by the shade of a nearby tree in that unexotic seaside tourist haven, with its five or seven ice cream parlors, stones that glittered enticingly from three or four jewelry stores, and T-shirts, soaps, model boats, and knickknacks of every kind, beckoning from the 12 or 15 tourist boutiques that lined the five-block town, brimming in summer, empty and icy in winter, or so they were told by a local musician, too attached to ever leave. None of it seemed to matter all of a sudden, and Adam himself was surprised by his dismay as he usually loved to go into town and pick out a book or, if luck came his way, a toy, with Mama's approving smile as she looked down at the coveted object he would clutch at Sherman's Department Store.

"I want to see Alice," he repeated matter of factly, knowing full well that she was far away. By the time his eyes met Emma's sympathetic gaze, he had already given in. "But how many more days till we go home?"

"What do you want to do this afternoon?" she countered in reply. He didn't answer, and probably didn't even hear his mother's question since the ice cream had taken up his attention and it was all he could do to keep up with the thick drips rolling down the sides of the cone. He walked toward the car, his sticky hand grasping Emma's, hoping that he could just go home and watch a movie, when he spied a boy in a swimsuit, running barefoot on the town green. Alice would never let me go barefoot like that, he thought, recalling the lawn at the Pitt Street pool, their chasing each other from tree to tree, and yelling "base" whenever they ran out of breath and were near a convenient elm. Adam laughed out loud as he thought of Alice screaming when he threw her shoe into the pool and how she dove in, resurfacing seconds later with the dripping footwear held high in victory. They were the first ones in the pool that Wednesday at the end of June, on a not-so-sunny day, unable to bear the anticipation a second longer. Adam was not exactly afraid of the water; he could actually stay in for hours if someone would just let him, but they were always saying that his "lips were turning blue"—which he thought a rather good color—and telling him to come out that instant and get warm. He considered this possibility himself when he waded into the ice-cold water with Alice by his side, muttering over and over that it was freezing, which made him worry that he might truly freeze and feeling too shy to ask her not to exaggerate.

It was much better when Alice took him on that long train ride to New Jersey, to Alice's pool in her own backyard, which was the perfect temperature. The whole ride long he was content to peer into his comic books despite Alice's chatter. But he could hardly believe his eyes when Jenna, Jason, Adeline (Alice's aunt), Granny and Gramps all rose from their sun bath to greet Adam who, at first, hid shyly behind Alice. By the end of the day he had them all in the pool, casting each one in their character of bad or good guy or girl, depending on the color of their suit: Red-O, Oranger, and WhiteOut were evil, and Greena, Yellowa, and Purpla were the super heroines. Resting for a moment at the side of the pool, Yellowa (Alice) found her thoughts wandering back to her childhood home, the tire swing that lifted her over the valley of the lawn, and her beloved Hattie barking in a mad chase to catch up to her; she would come so close, only to find the tire swing back out of range—like Rodger, Alice thought, swinging back to the present, and to Adam, who was leading her family of bathers with all the confidence of a theater director, his eyes bright pink with excitement and chlorine, his fingers shriveled at the tips from hours in the water, pointing to the other side of the pool. While the background was painful, the foreground was riveting, and she dove back into the water, immersing herself in the present and her love for the child.

With determined toes, Adam sprang from the edge of the pool towards Alice. How he screamed, each and every time, as if a world at once thrilling and terrifying would open up between them with every leap into her arms. "I never want to leave!" Adam yelled when she told him that they had to catch the 6 o'clock train back to the city. He watched her gather his action figures that were stationed strategically around the pool and ran out to help, wanting very much to please her.

"Do you want to go to Sand Beach?" she asked gaily. If there was one thing Emma was sure of, it was the allure of the ocean. He would undoubtedly load her basket with animal and superhero figures that they would place in the tower of a sandcastle, and around the moat: Batman would gaze out over the dip in the dune, and motion to Snow White that he would cross that gully of water as quickly as he could. Or they would throw Ironman into that same streamlet running from back in the woods, down the bank and through the dunes, and which puddled up peacefully a good 25 yards back from the roaring ocean. Ironman would stave off the rising tide flowing into the warm ochre paradise where the children played. He protected them from the mighty waves pounding on the shore with all the iciness of northern waters. Bee Hive Mountain loomed just beyond the watery meadow, where daring hikers—dotting the ascent with colorful backpacks—would hoist themselves onto the iron rungs till they reached the top. When Emma finally braved the climb, she practically puked from vertigo.

"Do you want to go to Sand Beach?" she asked again. He followed her distractedly to the car, fatigued from the morning's climb and the sunny afternoon. He sat quietly until Emma put on some Beatles music; soon they were both singing along to Ticket to Ride. They whirred lazily down Schooner Head Road, with Emma gazing at the trees bending windblown and pointing to Champlain Mountain that floated heavily on the other side of the marsh like an enormous rocky whale. Emma entered the drive with abandon, at home in the heavy salty air, the quiet road hugging the shore in the misty light, the Barred Owls making their way into the wooded expanse when it grew dark. She knew this winding way, sensually, and loved it most when her awareness fell away, when the ride back to the house became less painfully beautiful, and she could belt out a Beatles song with Adam for all the insects and toads to hear. But his look was wistful now, as if the beauty of the woods evoked for him the spirit of Alice, whispering through the trees. She let the quiet take hold, leaving him to his thoughts.

His mood turned with the turn onto the dirt road that bent around and down to the house. The grasses were bright at that hour, and the sea silver, capturing the breaks of light that streamed through an otherwise darkening sky, heavy with rain clouds some miles off. The Queen Anne's Lace and goldenrod danced down to the rocky shore where he typically skipped stones with his parents at the end of the day, secretly licking the polished grey granite, enchanted by the salty taste. Adam had high hopes of spotting a deer, a bear, or even a moose this time, and became so excited by a doe bolting out of the driveway that he practically fell out of the car when Emma turned off the motor. He slammed open the front screen door and ran into the house, yelling *Daaddyyy* with Emma trailing behind, arms filled with remnants of the day's adventures. They were greeted by a moan that rose groggily from the depths of a summer nap, and Emma could hear Luke yawn and roll back towards sleep. Adam's cranky eyes darted toward the TV, which he turned on in a flash. Anticipating an all-out war, Emma acquiesced when a talking sock puppet appeared on the screen, but it only seemed to make him mad.

"This is too *babyish!*" he yelled, stamping his foot. "I want to see another *Harry Potter!*" Luke had rented *The Sorcerer's Stone*, the first in the series, over Emma's adamant objections; and just as she had predicted, it was filled with violence, sadistic at times, all too much for a six-year-old. There was *quidditch*, a deadly game that had children soaring through the air, not knowing if they'd get the life whacked out of them, the teachers looking on, condoning the death match as spectators. Emma understood the necessity of magic in this world or any other; it was a child's only weapon against evil. She was taken by surprise when Adam declared that he liked the film, despite the cousin sprouting a pig's tail—which made him sick—and the final appearance of the villain Voldemort, whose head, Emma agreed, looked rather like a deflating balloon, zipping around the room, which was quite a relief after all those thick scenes of suspense that led up to his doom. Luke and Adam, huddled together on the couch, met her outraged look with defiance and tried to convince her that it really wasn't so bad.

"Adam, you can watch this puppet show or nothing," Emma declared without an inch for negotiation.

"Daddy will let me!" he stormed back, eyes glued, nevertheless, to the puppet bobbing merrily on the screen.

It was at moments like these, when Adam and Luke were aligned against her, that Emma really longed for Blacky, her beloved cat, who would sit quietly by and make the world seem like a graceful place to live in. There was an ache in the room, heavy with the boldness of her child and Luke's impatience. She cringed as if accused. Was she overly protective? He seemed eager to step into the life of his times. Unlike Luke, who was so directly engaged in the world around him, Emma felt distinctly out of step. She looked on at Adam, completely absorbed in the show. Or was he? He rose from the couch and slowly walked over to turn off the set; the sock puppets were now off the air. He crawled into Emma's arms in the tense silence of those who travel between worlds.

A few days later, back from town, Luke and Adam marched into the house, grinning fearlessly, with Adam waving *Harry Potter and the Prisoner of Azkaban* like a victory flag. He chattered away about the video store not having *The Chamber of Secrets*—the second in the series—so Daddy said it was okay to rent this one, the third, instead. So what if they watched it a little out of order, and could they please watch it *now*? Emma shot Luke a look. "It's rated PG," he said. "What could be so bad?"

Adam popped the disc into the DVD player and settled down to watch. "We'll turn it off if it gets too scary," Emma said.

"What are you scaring him for?" Luke snapped. Emma sank into the couch. Adam, oblivious, could hardly contain his excitement over the magical feats to come. Then he remembered that magic could transform things forever and became uneasy.

Emma noticed the strain of his smile when he asked: "It'll be good, right, Daddy?"

"Yes, of course," Luke answered absently, repositioning the TV set. Adam inched a little closer to him, and Luke wrapped a protective arm around his shoulder as the movie started.

Emma thought she might leave them to it. Eying her hiking boots near the door, she imagined herself on a vigorous circuit up and down Dorr Mountain. Yet something made her stay. She was more like Adam than she wanted to admit and felt compelled to watch Harry triumph once again. A boy who could outwit the murderous schemes of adults was the best sort of hero. She had to wonder if she didn't somehow harbor the same hope for Adam that she had for Harry, that he would somehow help change this terrible sad world. But wasn't it time that children be relieved of this task to transform all that's beastly by virtue of their innocence? Was its impact solely intended to thwart adult despair? Everybody wants to be rescued, adults, maybe, even more than children. Who wrote the story, after all? Not some child of eleven.

Emma was surprised that Adam got beyond the very first scene, with the awful Aunt Marge blowing up and sailing off into the night sky like a wailing beach ball. Adam was thoroughly nauseated by the image and shook with the force of Harry's spell. "Harry is good, isn't he?" he asked his father, needing reassurance.

"No one is all good or all bad," Luke responded wisely, and Adam persevered through the attack of the *dementors*, the ghostly prison guards that preyed like eerie jellyfish on people's fears. It was a purely medieval world, Emma thought, ordered by rituals of sacrifice and chivalry. She looked on in wonder as Adam bravely bore the execution of Buckbeak, the hippogriff—a creature half-bird, half-horse—who seemed to love Harry, and gave the boy his first taste of freedom as they sailed through the air, skimming over lakes and rising high in the sun-drenched sky, invulnerable—or so it seemed—to the shadowy craft of men. If anything in the film was meaningful to Emma, it was Harry's sympathy for Buckbeak, and the way the boy related to the animal world and it with him. But there was no justice here, and this was worrying Adam—Emma could tell—when poor Buckbeak succumbed to its cruel death. It was becoming increasingly clear that in this universe, the one you thought was friend was foe, and the enemy lurked not only without, but scariest of all, within.

There was nothing that Emma or Luke could have done to prepare Adam for the horror that now appeared before him. Adam had gathered from his own observations that the world was not altogether safe and did not want to accept it, let alone get used to it—which wasn't a bad thing, his father remarked.

"We should always feel indignant when someone's mean," Adam often recalled him saying. Once he understood what *indignant* meant, the more pressing matter was what to do with the feeling, which surely wasn't enough to make the situation better. The color would rise to his cheeks, but just when he turned to tell someone they were not being nice he would somehow freeze, and in seconds it would be too late. The only way to be effective, he observed, was to speak up right away. It was the time thing that bothered him most. If people would just wait till he got up the courage! Sometimes, he heard his voice snap back and shakily tell a mean kid to stop—like the other day when he saw Gordon throw a stone that missed Tom's face by a hair, he yelled out "hey!" and it was enough for Gordon to leave with his stupid friends. But most of the time, he could feel the other's hostility all too keenly, and it would stop him in his tracks, not that saying "hey" was any great feat, the child thought, shuddering from the incident.

But nothing he had ever seen or imagined could compare to the scene on the back hills of Hogwarts at midnight when the characters emerged from the dark world beneath the Whomping Willow. Adam had trouble following all the twists and turns of the plot but could surmise that in this world— and in his own—nothing was stable.

But no sooner had order been restored to their universe than it became undone under the glow of the full moon, which now peered out from behind the mountain, casting a pall over the vulnerable hill on which the children stood.

They all looked at the moon so fearfully, as did Adam; it was as if he were there, on that hill, Emma gathered from his white face and clenched muscles. And then it happened: the good teacher, Lupin, was gripped helpless by the moon, provoking the beast within him to burst through his very skin. His long, clawed feet stepping out of human shoes made the metamorphosis strangely real. Shaking his head under the grip of the transformation, from right to left, from right to left again, was all it took for the wolf's face to appear in place of his own. It was this seamless shift that appalled most, as if skin were but a bodily mask over an inner life with indeterminate qualities, and which threatened any sense of trust in others. There was Lupin, exposed, upright, naked in his close-cropped fur, the same light brown color as his hair, the last remnant of his human form. The transformation was complete, as the child soon realized. There was no more friendship here. Before their eyes was a creature of indiscriminate rage. Emma froze in place and watched the werewolf and Harry's protective godfather—now a black dog— leap against each other in attack, jaws and teeth sharply outlined against the night sky, heads thrown back, then thrust forward to gash, gnaw, and kill.

"*Mommy!*" Adam's voice was white as he rose in panic from the couch. Emma scooped him up in her arms and bolted up the stairs, as far away as possible from that scene of betrayal, where humans became what they feared most: a monstrous embodiment of madness, lunging to destroy the ones they loved.

"*I'm scared!*" Adam broke out again, too frightened to cry, move, or swallow.

"Luke, would you turn that *off!*" Emma yelled down at him, surprised that he hadn't followed them.

"Bring him down! I know he'll feel better if he sees how it ends, and it's gotta have a happy ending! Harry's the hero!" he yelled back confidently.

She supposed he was right, in theory anyway, and viewing it herself some months later, she had to admit that the narrative was truly compelling. Like Harry, Emma was also attuned to what felt like a lurking life, revealing itself to her in certain kinds of light, certain strains of silence, certain moods or atmospheres. For Emma, this was relational phenomena, as it was for Harry; but her domain was the non-human world, vegetables or trees. She could relate to them in ways she never thought possible, and it was the stuff of her drawings. This poignant otherness most startled her when she sensed it in the inanimate world. One of her very favorite paintings, Fortuna's *Interior Life of Stones*, gave entry into the blue chips of granite and its twinkling stars and tentacled fault lines; those silent stones were imbued with cosmic aliveness. Emma was overcome at times by such revelations. She would also recoil from the power of such things. A pencil or piece of paper could make her shudder at the proximity of mineral life in all of its non-living essence. But as terrifying as this could be, there was no doubt that it was subtler, and less threatening, than the forms of bestial-human aggression that had appeared on the screen.

The idea of subjecting Adam (or herself, for that matter) to one more second of those violent images made her refusal absolute, and widened what she privately called the "media gulf" between herself and Luke. He accused her of being childish in so utterly believing what she saw on the screen. But if art didn't ask us to suspend disbelief, she retorted during one of their innumerable arguments on the subject, what good was it? She was helpless as a spectator in the throes of horror. She wondered how Luke could be moved by something if he remained outside of it, always conscious of the level of mere representation, mere fiction. Didn't he want *his* audience to enter into the illusion of his drama? Luke countered that suspension of disbelief was a willful act, not a loss of reality testing. Could Emma not see that? No, she couldn't, actually; she wholly entered a work of art—but not just any work of art; it had to be powerful—in the same way, she entered a dream by validating the parameters of that universe. The couple never could get past this point of mutual incomprehension, and Emma would come away filled with self-doubt about her intolerance of fictive horror, yet still preferring her responsiveness to Luke's rational detachment. But then, what to do about life, which was a horror, too? Scream and run? In any event, Adam, being six, couldn't make such clear distinctions between art and life, fantasy and reality, especially when he was terrified, and she suspected that no amount of rational discussion of such subjects would ever shake his sense that metamorphosis was not just possible but far more terrible than he had thought. And she had to agree if by metamorphosis Adam meant—and she knew that he did mean—the radically altering effect of aggression, completely catching you off-guard.

For the next 48 hours, Adam didn't sleep and could barely swallow. He wouldn't leave Emma's side, and demanded that she stay near him, especially when he had to use the bathroom, where he felt most vulnerable. During the day, it was almost bearable to be alive, but as night fell, the moon terrified him, and he distrusted the whole sky, fearing its transformative power. He would clutch at himself to contain the beast that might break through the walls of his skin. He felt better when he was in the town of Bar Harbor; it was the closest thing to New York City. But The Cove—their remote house by the sea—was too much like Hogwarts castle, so close to the natural world and to the water, and just because Adam had watched *Harry Potter and the Prisoner of Azkaban* in that living room. Emma tried everything she could think of to convince him he was safe, but he kept saying, as kindly as he could: "Mama, I know you're trying, but it's just not working!" and begged her to take him back to the city, where there were no foothills or shadowy forests amid those concrete towers, and werewolves never set foot.

Luke was horrified that they might go home early. He needed the break even more than he had realized. Besides, there was a good ten days left before they had to leave. But he could not bear to watch Adam suffer, and walked around feeling alternately sheepish about having rented the movie in the first place, yet convinced that, had Adam seen it to the end, he would have been able to better accept the scary scene because order had been restored in Harry's universe. Why did Emma have to be so dramatic? Her reaction might have bolstered Adam's fears. As if responding to that suspicion, Emma, desperate after two nights of her vigil, and the endless Beatles songs that she sang to Adam until dawn, begged Luke to tell Adam how the movie ended. But it turned out to be incomprehensible, even for Emma. There was something about Hermione existing in the future and the present at the same time, which somehow seemed to mean that wizardry eventually undid the deaths of the innocents— Buckbeak, and Sirius Black, the godfather—who, in the end, flew away together into the unbound skies above Hogwarts.

Adam didn't buy it. "But they *did* die!" he exploded. "I *saw* it happen! They *killed* Buckbeak! And what about Lupin? Did he change back into a professor forever?"

Luke had to admit that a werewolf he would always remain. This infuriated Adam since he so badly wanted to see that spell undone and bury forever Lupin's metamorphosis into a vicious beast under the full moon, which happened once a month! He threw his Batman toy across the room in frustration, and its arm broke off when it hit the Formica table. Luke bit his lip, and Adam, seeing his father so sad and upset, set about consoling him. But his little body gave way under the strain, and he fell into Emma's arms exhausted and slipped at last into a long and dreamless sleep.

He awoke later that day, ravenous. Emma cut up an apple, which he bit into eagerly, then gave her a strange look, with—was it possible? blood oozing over his lip. The feral picture startled her; Adam, stamping his foot, drew back from her uncomprehending gaze.

"My tooth, Mama! My front tooth!" Emma ran to get some ice. But where was the tooth?

"It's just like *One Morning in Maine*, 'cause I'm six, like Sal, but I really don't want to be *just* like her, 'cause she lost *her* tooth looking for clams, and that would be *terrible* if I couldn't find *mine*! I can't wait to have a visit from the tooth fairy!"

They started searching the room, soon joined by Luke, who, determined to do right by Adam, soon found the tooth and held it up with a triumphant wave. Adam jumped into his arms, happy for the first time in days. Emma would be forever grateful to the little fairy who had ended Adam's terror and, as they drove into town for a chocolate ice cream cone (just like Sal had), devised a plan to keep him feeling safe. What he needed was a *heart guard*—another name for a breastplate—she told him the next morning. His eyes lit up, and, within the hour, she and her young knight were leaving *Sherman's* department store. Bedecked in a silver suit of armor, replete with copper trim and insignia, he held his shield in front of him with one hand, and his sword thrust forth with the other, ready to conquer the moon.

Adam insisted on wearing the whole costume—helmet included—to bed that night. Eyes wide open, on his back, he gripped his sword that lay defiantly on his chest like a cross: *a double heart guard*, he explained to Emma. It was weeks before he would agree to face the night without his armor, but slept with that sword on his chest well into December.

The following morning, Adam awoke to a rustling beneath his pillow. He pulled out a *Fantastic Four* comic book, with this note:

Dear Adam,

Thank you so much for the beautiful tooth. I will keep it always. Here is a gift in exchange, which I hope you will love.

Look out the window when the sun goes down, and you will see twinkling in the trees. That will be me, watching over you. I will return every night that you are here at The Cove to keep you safe. You will see me, but your parents cannot because only children can see fairies.

Your friend,
The Tooth Fairy

Adam was beside himself with joy and growing confidence as Emma read it to him, and he was soon running around the porch, talking with the trees about his new secret and slaughtering demons with his sword. Emma, through some magic of her own, having found the way to rescue Adam from the threat of metamorphic beasts, decided to reward herself with a climb up Cadillac Mountain, which for years she had dreamed of scaling. Luke and Adam drove her to the foot of South Ridge Trail and left with the promise to meet her at the top in three hours' time. It was no problem for Luke, who loved the drive up into the clouds, nor for Adam, who had a fondness for the gulls that hung about the peak.

He wondered how those sea birds flew up so high to scavenge contentedly in the parking lot of Cadillac Mountain. They floated about in the wind, as if dangling from the clouds; and when they landed on the pink stone wall on the edge of the parking lot, they were completely unafraid of him as he stepped gently closer to them. This was the closest he had ever come to an animal that wasn't a pet, and he loved to study the snowy white feathers and perfect gray wings with their blackened tips. The bird was perfect in every way, but the beak was so strange, with that thick black band around the yellow bill. Did that keep it shut? Adam stretched out a hand to pull it off, and the gull screeched indignantly, which made him laugh. He sure could open that mouth! Adam looked closely at its bright yellow eye and the orangey-red ring distinctly encircling it, with that same orange-red outlining the back of the gull's beak. What a color, almost like bright blood, but the bird did not look hurt. In fact, it was now fiercely eyeing *him*. The child stared back in silence for what felt like an eternity, until the gull broke into shrill laughter, and Adam jumped and screeched himself. It was he who looked away. The vivid ring around that eye conveyed a fearlessness that this young knight could never match.

Emma started up the mountain trail, the air thick with mist from the morning rain. The first part of the climb wound up through woods so dark that she could hardly see the sky. Something here was alive, breathing almost, in the moss and the mud. She left a trail of muddy prints as she traveled over the unsteady bog walks, which she noticed with dismay as she looked back. What she wanted was to lose track of herself, not to be seen by anyone, least of all herself. All she ever wanted was to be *of things*, to subsist as a crackle upon twigs, a tripping amid dead leaves, a mere upright creature, without the consciousness of being one.

But there was something in the way—faint at first, then gradually blocking out all other sound. It was her heart, pounding so loud that she was sure she heard it as she wandered up the trail through those deep woods. The bird calls got fainter, and she felt nervous in the growing silence. Now she thought she didn't want this unfamiliar solitude. But her boots had taken on a life of their own, persevering steadily, despite her fear. Out might suddenly spring a red fox, or a black bear might be there at the next turn, ready to attack. The crack of twigs and tumbling scree increased her vigilance. Soon her clothes were soaked with sweat. She strained to see what she imagined Eagle's Crag would look like, where the first marker of the trail up the incline was posted, but it was nowhere in sight. Was she actually wishing this hike were over? She decided to trust her boots; they didn't seem to care.

It was Emma's first real adventure since Adam was born and with this realization her reverie resumed as she wandered more calmly up the mountainside. What had made her so afraid? The contrast with the person she once was— daring, some said, always curious about the unfamiliar— startled her. Luke had come into her life or, rather, she'd slid fast into his, grabbed by the ankles into the undertow that threw her into a place of crude passion. The first time she saw him there was something raw and looking for love that haunted her for days. And she felt it still, this undertow... it made her reveal herself in ways so yielding that she would have been embarrassed had she not felt so at home with this man. But it scared her, nevertheless, to exist so close to her thrill and terror.

She looked for him in places close to death, and even there she would find him. Her fourth miscarriage had sent her spiraling into darkness, as if she were dying with the infant she had lost. Night after night, she awoke with a gasp, the wind snatched from her lungs. Luke would grab her back into this world and sit up with her until she could brave sleep again. She had given up, unable to bear another loss. And it was precisely at that moment that Adam was conceived.

Some seven months after his birth, when the first plane hit the Tower, the soundscape of the city changed forever. After that, every time a jet would cross the sky, Emma heard *that* plane. But on that morning, oddly, she heard nothing—not the screams in Washington Square, not the hum of shock that followed, not the squirrel digging its way into a nearby stroller bag. She had been nursing Adam, their gazes locked in quiet union. Then a woman ran breathless into the baby park where Emma sat alone with Adam and pointed towards the World Trade Center. Emma looked south, saw the smoking tower, and froze. She never knew for how long. Minutes? An hour? Finally, she stood up, barely able to make her way home, pushing the stroller with one hand, holding Adam close with the other. His intelligent body sensed her fear, and she could have sworn that he was trying to get her attention with repeated gurgles and coos to steady her in his small, powerful way. He even grabbed her chin and turned it towards him, insisting that she look at him. But when she looked back again, she saw it—not straight on but in the eyes of others—the collapse of that first tower. She saw people screaming, their mouths open, but she did not hear them. The sound of that day was something she invented as she tried to make sense of the thing, days, months, years later when other planes would fly over the city.

The pressure of the moment stripped everything of its meaning; she could not feel the vibrations rippling across the city like an unearthly earthquake. The waves simply did not hit her. She held Adam for hours, could not put him down. Neither mother nor infant seemed able to move. The last feeding had occurred at the time of the crash, much earlier that morning. At last, overcome by hunger, he cried for her. And *that* she heard, in real time and in memory. She cringed as his two bottom teeth dug into her nipple. She tried again, several times, through that night and into the morning until she could bear it no longer. The work of 9/11 was so personal, so intimate, disrupting the primordial link between them. Adam could no longer nurse without biting her. He associated feeding with the panic that shot through them when that stranger slammed open the gate to the baby park—a sound that he heard all too well and which jolted Emma into looking up to see the woman's terror-stricken face, her shaking fingers pointing south. Emma had no choice but to wean Adam early, marking their first separation.

She withdrew in the years that followed, not in any noticeable way, and certainly not from Adam, and not from Luke, either, who read to her every night: *Walden Pond*, then *Anna Karenina*, followed by Mrs. Gaskell's *Wives and Daughters*, till she could once again bear certain kinds of silence. Slowly she regained her buoyancy, bounding down the street as she once did, portfolio under her arm, always ready to stop and talk to the familiar faces she ran into. And yet she knew that she no longer moved through the world as she had done before that day. But now, though, she reckoned that she had been somehow readying herself, all these years, for a good climb up a mountain.

It wasn't till she crossed the Feather Bed that the sun broke through the trail—the trees had now practically disappeared. Her footing was freed from the forest's sinking clay as she made her way up the pink granite ridge. Now, at the summit, impenetrable boulders held her high. She turned to look back down the path she'd traveled, then back out again at the view— stunned at the sight of the rippling peaks, the smaller sisters of Cadillac—Champlain and Dorr—plunging their sides low into the ocean bed, disappearing in the deep. She sat on the bald granite pier jutting out into the sky, gazing with the simplicity of exhaustion, a tired, older goddess, in the midst of her longing.

PART TWO

I. Alice

The ringing broke a solemn mood that had taken hold of Alice, like a shadow creeping through her, unrelenting, for the past month. Something light and faintly fluttery would rise up suddenly when she was down in this distraction, only to fade in the moments that followed, dashing the dimmest hope that she would ever get over losing Rodger. The fact that he was no longer near—that he was, in fact, truly gone— was replaced by something still more disquieting, which she could only describe as an eerie dissimilitude, by which she meant that either she never really knew Rodger, or that he'd undergone some profound change that she had never noticed. Both possibilities were equally perplexing. She would lie in her room for hours, staring up at a faint crack in the paint that had somehow made its way along a good three-quarters of the ceiling, and which had revealed itself one night when she was pondering the relationship. A few days prior, she had received a big box in the mail full of belongings she had left in his apartment. They still breathed of intimacy but fell limp in her hands as she searched for a note, a sign, anything at all until she reached the bottom of the box. She was much too sad to fight her way back out of that emptiness, but still kept struggling to make sense of it all, as if locating the cause of the fissure, figuring out how it had spread across her ceiling, then stemming it once and for all would put a stop to the insidious crack that had wound its way through reality, leaving her in a perpetual state of disbelief.

She wasn't altogether sure if she had done the right thing by moving home for the summer. Jenna, shocked at seeing her daughter a good fifteen pounds thinner in just three weeks, insisted that Alice come to New Jersey after Adam left for Maine, and sat in her daughter's apartment with her, aching to help her find relief from the pain as Alice slowly packed her bags. Jenna was convinced that Alice needed nurturing to recover, and that everything would take care of itself if she would just come home.

After the separation and divorce from Hank, Jenna, in a low-lying but pervasive state of shock, lost her footing, and with it, her influence, her very sense of motherhood, which had been such a stable, integral facet of her identity ever since Alice was born. For a time, if her daughter didn't outright reject her mother's counsel, she would simply ignore it. Then Jenna met Jason, and Alice's world turned sideways with the imperative of adjusting to a new home, and in it, a *stepfather* (the word sounded crooked, as if on crutches. But he was truly nice, which was a relief, and Alice was content to just call him *Jason*. No one but Alice, with the exception of Jason himself, felt the hint of affection in the inflection of his name as she lingered, for a second more, over the long *A*, a subtle intonation that asserted itself over time, and he was sensitive to it). Alice would try to do her best in this new world, but it was a lot. And Jenna knew it. Some wounds take a long time to heal, if ever. She learned about them in nursing school: the body could mostly take care of itself, apart from those wounds that became chronic. But this one was emotional and of a totally different order. She recalled Harry's devastation upon discovering Josie's betrayal of him in *Twin Peaks*. He loved her so that the shock was unbearable, and it made emotional sense that the character did not reappear in the third season, *The Return*, so aptly entitled, and which resonated with a kind of *no-return*—for characters who came too dangerously close to the truth, like the General, whose head would forever hang like a planet in the sky, for Dale who was cast out of time, seemingly forever, having gone too far in his attempt to right the atrocities that had befallen Laura Palmer—and in the poignant absence of Harry, too sick (at heart?) to be restored to the world. Jenna pushed these images from her mind; she didn't want to land in fear. She would pick herself up and go on, no matter what. Things were precarious with her daughter: if only Alice would let her be her mother again—in the fullest sort of way—then even this wound would heal. It was her hope, anyway.

It was probably for the best, Alice reflected, that she not stay in the City. Who knew what loneliness awaited her there? But back in her New Jersey den, she felt daily twinges of rebellion as she realized, with regret, that she could no longer come home, in the deep sort of way. And while her body regressed into a thing that must be fed, she found that she couldn't swallow. This had nothing to do with the tonsillectomy (she could barely recall the pain of the operation), but with the heavy regret that had formed a permanent lump in her throat. As it was, it was hard to know what to hold onto; she didn't dare swallow up what was left.

Although the house now felt remote, there was still a place where she could feel the old connection: the garden. Digging among the flowers gave her unexpected relief, as if the tension of sorrow made its way through her arms and expelled itself through her fingers into the dark soil. From sun-up till sundown, Alice weeded even the thickest confines of the yard, barely conscious of her ripped cuticles (she insisted on gardening without gloves), the grassy stains on her legs, and the scrapes on her knees from days of kneeling, as if in continual prayer to Gaia, who answered by yielding up the endless roots of ragweed, dandelion, nettle, pigweed, bittercress and thistles that gave the weakened gardener a glimmer of triumph when, at the end of a long, fastidious clearing, she would fall withered, yet content, onto the grass. The smells of the upturned dirt and hot summer blooms did more than infuse, linger and surround. They consumed her, and Alice would let go one of those pent-up sighs and unburden herself. A precocious firefly would come flitting ahead of its brothers, warning her that twilight was near so that if she dared linger, the mosquitoes would pinch her in irritation and chase her inside. She would slam the door in frustration but vaguely relieved—it was hard work—from that all-too-brief taste of repose.

It was at one of those moments, in an early evening in late July, after the first mosquito had managed to bite through her jeans (leaving a welt, square on her knee, that swelled with an annoying itch from her constant kneeling), that Alice, grumpy from her imminent exile from the garden, distinctly heard her cell phone ringing all the way up in her bedroom. She was usually so deep in thought or buried in her grim mood those weeks that she practically never heard the ring, but this time it caught her attention, and she bounded up the stairs as if responding to an emergency. She caught it at the last, just before it switched to her voice mail. On the other end was a voice distinctly recognizable, but so small that there was something weird about it.

"It's Adam."

"Adam! It's Alice! Are you okay?" There was an uncharacteristic silence on the other end of the line, and she thought that she could hear some crying.

"What's the matter?"

"It's the werewolf, and the black dog, and the moon!"

"What werewolf? Is Mommy there?" she asked in sympathetic terror. How Adam might've encountered the threatening bunch? in a book? or a dream? Well, if Emma was there, surely there was no reason for alarm.

"Yes, Mommy's right here. The werewolf was in the TV, but I think he comes here when it's nighttime."

"Oh, you saw him on TV?"

"Not really *on* TV; it wasn't a show. It was a movie that we put *into* the TV: *Harry Potter III*. That's the one with the werewolf. Did you see it?"

"I only saw the first one. But don't worry. The werewolf can't hurt you. He only lives in the movie."

"He does?"

"Yes, he can't get out of there."

"But what if he finds a way? Well, even if he does, the tooth fairy will protect me."

"Is she there?"

"Yes, she's right outside, in the trees. Can you see her twinkling? She's protecting the house."

"Do you think that she could come to my backyard?"

"NO! She said that she was staying here until I leave so I won't be scared. Maybe she can come to you when I come home from Maine."

"Oh, good! I could use a little protecting myself."

"Why? Is there a werewolf in your backyard?"

"No," she answered laughing, but quickly refrained, having understood that Adam had been very frightened. "It's that I would just love a visit from the tooth fairy, that's all," she continued. "I've had my grown-up teeth for a while, and it's been a long time since the fairy came to see me that—wait a minute! Does that mean that you've lost a tooth?"

"Yes! My other front tooth! It fell out while I was eating an apple, and we were so scared that we wouldn't be able to find it like Sal, but Daddy found it, and we went to town to get ice cream and a knight's costume."

"Wow, that's so exciting!"

"The ice cream was good, but I don't think it was so exciting. I don't like losing anything, especially body parts."

"I know, it feels strange, but a new tooth will come in, and it will be like you hadn't lost anything after all."

"Well, I *did* lose my *baby* tooth. But Mommy said that the tooth fairy was keeping it in a special place for me, so it isn't really lost. So I guess I didn't lose it because I know where it is."

"Adam, it's so great to hear your voice. I really miss you!"

"I really miss you, too. Mommy says we're coming home in 6 days, and I hope to see you right away. Will you come to my house?"

"Yes, of course I'll come. Right away!"

Adam was probably the person Alice liked most to be with, and it wasn't until she heard his voice that she realized just how much she missed him, and how she fell into darkness not long after he left for Maine. His imminent return made her more hopeful, and the week ahead didn't seem so dreadfully long. She ran down the steps, ravenous, and attacked the lasagna that Jenna had been cooking the day before. She was too hungry to reheat it and guzzled a long draught of Coke, which gave her a sugary buzz. Jenna had wandered into the kitchen while the feast was underway and startled Alice with one of her own pent-up sighs. She hugged her daughter from behind, careful not to let Alice see her tears of relief. The two had known many moments of unhappiness together, but the look on her daughter's face lately was unlike anything she had ever seen. There was something far away about it, and her losing all that weight intensified the mother's feeling that Alice was fading away. She caught herself missing Alice even though she was in the house.

As if in response, Alice reached back to draw her mother down toward her for a quick hug, not wanting to give into the emotion, which would frankly ruin her dinner, the first she'd eaten with gusto since the summer began, though it was just a little pasta. It was a start. Jenna pulled up a chair as Alice told her about Adam, *Harry Potter*, and the werewolf. His fright preoccupied her. She could get inside the way the child saw the world as it felt so much like her own, in its intense indignation, joy or sadness. Alice felt at home in his presence—preferring it perhaps to Jenna's, and this made her flinch with guilt. As she took in her mother's old delicious smell of verbena, Alice felt the flush of what life would be like without her and was terrified. Surviving the loss of Rodger was causing her to molt (which is how she put it to herself)—a kind shedding from within of a lingering threat, which disrupted her connection with herself and with the world. She saw that Adam too felt under threat, and wanted to somehow impart to him her hope that together they might find themselves again, free, of incapacitating fear or the kind of sadness that pulled you under.

Jenna commented that the best possible thing for the little boy was to have fun and feel like his old self again—and Alice's thoughts went right to the ocean. That was it! She would take Adam to the beach! She would get up early and take him on the train to Spring Lake (she was sure Emma would agree), where she had spent many a raucous moment at the water's edge, thrilled by the waves which grew higher as the day grew longer, crashing with froth and salt at her feet. She could never tear herself away and, even at the age of 5, would dare herself to slip loose from her father's grasping hand and take just one step closer to the breaking tide. She would run toward the watery horizon and wait for his swooping arms to grab her from behind and feel his peals of laughter fall all over her. It was precisely the untamed part of herself that her father loved most, or, on reflection, could most connect to. As time went on, the more she tried to fit in socially, the more remote he became, missing in her—and in himself—that capacity for wild delight. Was it still lurking somewhere? Had her father left their home because he had finally given up, or because he wanted that last chance to find himself? And what had he found, after all those years? Alice drew a blank, but was not sure if this was due to the quality of Hank's lonely existence, or to his absence, in herself.

It was one of those days that were so soft and breezy that even Hank, sour and stumbling from a vague hangover, couldn't help but take heart in the airy feel of it, to the point that he actually heard himself mutter, "What a beautiful day!" He made a strong cup of coffee and found himself sipping it, in his boxers and T-shirt, under a willow, looking up at a robin perched just overhead, then beyond to some puffy clouds that looked like a dragon, but which soon melted into a dolphin diving back into the ocean. "Maybe the little house isn't so bad after all," he thought, as the screen door to the kitchen swung ajar, then returned to its place with a mild slam, in a courteous sort of way. Despite himself, he had grown attached to the place, even though the paint was chipping inside and out, and its rooms hung low with his long, angry moods. After the divorce, he'd spent his last dollar on the place, suspicious of his growing restlessness that might, if he wasn't careful, find him homeless. It was, he conceded, an attempt to provide for himself when all else seemed lost. And while he chose a place that had an extra bedroom, he had no romantic fantasies of new beginnings. And he rather liked being on his own, without all the tense expectations hanging over him. Still, he felt strongly that there should be a room for Alice, although it never occurred to her to stay over. In fact, he never asked. The room remained a last link to civilization, where he thought, vaguely, that he could be something to somebody.

Why he felt inclined to weed that morning, he didn't know; it hadn't occurred to him that whole spring and summer to do something about the dandelions that had invaded the stone path, which wound its way from the porch into the far reaches of the yard. Hank had decided to buy the house because of that path; it had a mystery about it, with those blue flowers that peered delicately over the old stones. "That's blue star creeper," the real estate agent replied, as if in response to Hank's charmed gaze, and, finding the agent sympathetic, he sealed the deal right then and there. He allowed himself those impetuous gestures. They gave him the satisfaction of defiance when they weren't altogether stupid. In this case, luck had it that the house was structurally sound and the roof was in excellent condition. Besides the paint job that it sorely needed, it was something of a gem. The house was really more like a cottage; it was small indeed—but this suited him fine, since it felt less suburban, and the acres of yard made it all seem more native—and a bit windblown, which appealed to his sensibility. It had the character of a place that had been lived in, and Hank rather liked the unpretentious neighborhood and the fact of its being not too far from the ocean, although he rarely went.

Before he knew it, he was poking around the garage in search of a hoe to attack those dandelions rooted beneath the stones, tangled in the roots of the star creeper, and which were frankly pissing him off. The shade of the garage did him good, as the afternoon sun was beating down and, despite the breeze, beginning to make him woozy. He wasn't in the habit of bending over for so long. But he would be damned if he would let those weeds destroy his blue flowers, and he raged a bit about how foolish he had been not to have paid closer attention. It was his fault, after all, that he had merely stood by, taking little notice of the yellow blossoms, which, unattended, had graduated into fluffy white balls (*parachutes*, Alice used to call them) that spread their seeds by the thousands all over his yard. Soon Hank's brow and T-shirt were soaked with sweat, and his back was aching from the chore, but he was having trouble tearing himself away as he had only tackled half the path, and was determined to show them, at the last, who was boss. With stomach growling, he clutched the hoe and sank its blade into the hardened earth around the stones and soon was making headway, satisfied by the fruits of his labor.

As he didn't hear the car door slam, he was jolted by the rattle of the gate. No one ever came to see him and, since he usually went into the yard from the kitchen, it was a sound he seldom heard. He turned to find Alice gazing at him in admiration. He replied with one of his rare smiles and opened his one free arm as if awaiting a hug. She stood shyly, or wary, perhaps, that the gesture wasn't meant for her and, sensing her hesitation, he walked over and gave her a sweaty kiss, his stubbly face brushing her youthful cheek.

"I'm way too gross for a hug," he said in apology, feeling unusually grateful for the visit. "Want to get some breakfast?"

Alice laughed in that deep way she had, pointing to her watch as if to say: "Are you joking? It's three o'clock!" to which he responded that he had been too busy weeding to have time to eat. It was then that he noticed her knees, sticking out all knobby-like, badly bruised and green around the edges, and she rewarded him with another peal of laughter.

"I've been gardening, too!" She didn't want to say it was a matter of survival, so left it at that. Her father did a double-take and looked back down at her knees. It wasn't that they were knobby but actually *boney*, and his gaze made its way back up her body, and he considered with attention her hip bones, shoulder blades, and rib cage that jutted through her jean shorts and T-shirt. He took in her suffering but asked no questions, and Alice, who had read his thoughts, was grateful for his silence.

"Let's get some breakfast, okay? I just want to take a quick shower, and then we'll go into town. There's a new little place that isn't half bad with excellent bacon and eggs and pancakes. You'll love it." And he dashed inside, leaving Alice to her thoughts.

Alice made her way over to the willow and was stirred by the activity of the place, the butterflies in chaotic flight, and the hundreds of bees having a bash in the overgrown flower-beds. Well, she could always come over here for the rest of the week, since she'd just about finished her mother's yard. It gave her some relief to know there was still work to be done before Adam came home, at which point she'd move back into the city. But as she gazed across the lawn and her eyes fell on the tangled thickets, she reconsidered: the yard had a soul of its own in the overrun way that was so like her father, with those careless vines flowering despite his neglect, and the cobbled path and marbled nymph whose steady arms held up a bath for the chickadees, its smile erupting suddenly through light-green lichens. No doubt her father liked it this way, untamed and inviting a romp. Her mother and Jason had an entirely different approach. Their lawn was preened and pruned, and the poolside immaculate. Such order also appealed to Alice; she took solace in the predictability of the thing. But she had to admit it was devoid of charm, except for the wooden fence, which made for a good sitting spot for a beer with Rodger, now gone from her, probably for good, yet still haunting her all the same, like so many things.

It occurred to Alice, as she sat under the willow, that, on the face of it, her parents had divorced because of her father's drinking, his fugues. But there was this undercurrent, stronger than all the rest, that better explained the fissure in their relationship and which came down to their wildly different sensibilities. This was clear from their houses. Her mother had settled in a nest both manicured and safe, while her father went for the unkempt, unshaven, rough but charming place. Such is who each one had always been. Alice gazed back to the winding path, the hoe, and the pile of weeds off to the side, baking in the sun. It tickled her to see her father take care of something, and she wondered if he would actually finish the job, as quite a stretch of weedy stone lay waiting. That was her father: spontaneous, passionate, and incapable of following through. The thought of it almost made her want to leave to preserve his warm welcome, as he might turn cold and remote by the end of the day.

She stood up bravely as the kitchen door slammed, and Hank strode out, keys in hand. He opened the gate and motioned her to come along. She came to him in silence, keeping to herself the wish to weed. He noticed her cautious step and smiled back (the second time that day) to reassure her. She found herself refusing his offer to wash up before they left, lest she find something disturbing in the house on her way to the bathroom—too many dirty dishes in the sink, liquor bottles on the floor, a mad dog lurking in the shadows. And what else? Her father turning into a werewolf at the next full moon? She smiled at her affinity with Adam, and her father, misreading her look, thought Alice condescending with that refusal, and it ruffled his feathers. So what if the house was a mess? Ever vigilant, she sensed his shift in mood and blurted out that they should get going; she was half-starved—and from the look of things, this was probably true, Hank had to admit, and calmed down. The idea of Alice eating heartily in his presence made him hurry, and it gave him pause to find himself feeling so paternal. They tucked themselves into Hank's red Chevy and were soon belting out "Red Rubber Ball," one of his favorites, which he'd taught Alice when she was a toddler. At that time, it delighted her to think of the sun as a bouncing ball, unaware that it was a song of separation that she and her father had been singing throughout her childhood, but which now felt vaguely hopeful with this bouncing back after the fall she had taken in the split up with Rodger.

They pulled up to Hank's new joint, *The Busy Bee*, and Alice felt a rare joy just to be with him and unconsciously mimicked his oddly confident stride up the stairs. Her mouth watered unexpectedly from the smells of bacon and syrup that hung around the perimeter of the place. The fact that this restaurant served only breakfast suited Hank. He loved to imagine it sizzling and souffléing at his pleasure, any time of day or night. He was met with friendly greetings as he stepped inside. Two cute waitresses came flocking to him. He was handsome, Alice knew, but thoughts of his intimate life—if he had one—were disconcerting, not just because he was her father, but because of what she'd had with Rodger, and her intense fantasies of him that preoccupied her so much of the day, making her feel broken and craven. Alice noticed the waitress's looks of wonder as her father led her by the hand to his favorite booth by the window.

"Sue, Michelle, this is my daughter, Alice," Hank announced proudly.

"Happy to meet you, darlin'," Sue chimed, turning to Hank with a gaze of disbelief. "Hank, you never told us you had a daughter! She's a beauty! Just like her father, with those deep dark eyes."

That he had never mentioned her, or even *thought* of it, miffed Alice (it never occurred to her that his silence on the subject could have come from his sense of failure as a father. She would've never guessed that he might suffer in this way, absorbed as she was by his apparent rejection of her throughout her childhood), but Sue's comment made her feel close to him all the same, as if the waitress had uncovered some mysterious link between them. As far back as she could remember, nobody ever compared Alice to Hank or pointed out any sort of likeness, physical or otherwise, as if such an affinity would steer her into the ways of the unconventional or, God forbid, disreputable. She never thought of herself as her father's child, but the idea of it pleased her, not because she wanted to be like him, but because it anchored her somewhere else. Feeling like a stranger in her mother's house was getting hard to take. Despite her mother's good intentions, Alice felt smothered, and wondered vaguely if that was how Hank too had felt when he lived there with them. With the collapse of her relationship with Rodger, recovering any sense of self, rooted in a life, a past, or even a present, felt impossible. There was nowhere to go but elsewhere; and for that moment, her father, who had taken it upon himself to order her a stack of blueberry pancakes and a side of bacon—her all-time favorite breakfast—seemed like a viable, albeit unnerving, option.

"I can't eat another bite," said Alice a half-hour later, letting her syrupy fork fall beside her plate. She hadn't even known that she was hungry, but when their order came, it was all she could do not to drool with delight. Hank glowed as he watched his daughter eat, down to the last mouthful, as she told him all about her art classes, teachers, and Adam. Was it really because of him, his being there with her, that she was eating? He dared not bring up the subject of her weight, as it would spoil the moment, but decided he would call Jenna later that day and find out how long this had been going on. He was both surprised by his intention (he rarely spoke to Jenna, and only when *she* called *him*), and somewhat irked by the fact that Jenna hadn't told him what Alice had been going through. Oh well, Alice is no longer a child; she probably would have told me about it sooner or later, he reflected, so attentively that he actually uttered the words, "sooner or later."

"Sooner or later what?" Alice asked.

Searching quickly for an answer, he hastily replied, "Sooner or later get to the beach."

"Oh!... you actually want to go to the beach? With me?"

While that hadn't been his intention at all, he didn't want to hurt her feelings and proposed that they at least take a walk on the boardwalk, and why not go right away?

And there they were, gliding slowly down Ocean Avenue (there was always traffic in the summer, but no one ever minded much, what with the waves so loud that they seemed to pound on the car roof, and the smell of hot suntan lotion infusing the air with its delicious heaviness), hugging the very shore of those childhood memories that stirred Alice with regret. Her father's thick quiet signaled his own stirrings, but he was more relaxed with silence than she ever was, and she sought to mimic his comfort with it, stealing closer to him in that wordless hour, imagining their bond, just as she did growing up. She was so like her mother, usually chattering about this or that, going over countless details of a party, a boyfriend, a hockey game that filled the childhood house with intermittent moments of joy.

While Hank had a quiet way to begin with, his silence became a sort of weapon, rising like a wall as the years passed, splitting the den, the kitchen, even the front stoop with a deafening presence. Alice would walk through that wall with trepidation, moving in turn toward her father or her mother. Their sorrow, their hurt, was for each so different in texture and mingled in Alice in ways so disconcerting at times that it was all she could do not to parachute herself out the window to escape the clutches of their mutual incomprehension. How had it come to that? She had spent hours of her high school years looking at the wedding photo that sat stupidly on the piano long after everyone knew it was over. Their love was like velvet, Alice used to say to herself as a child whenever she looked at that photograph. Both Jenna's and Hank's eyes were dark and deep to the point that one could say they were black, but soft and filled with inviting. By the time Alice reached eleventh grade, she could barely look at the photograph, let alone into the eyes of Jenna or Hank, or anyone else's for that matter. There was one exception: the horse Juniper, down at Millicent's farm. Its nonhuman gaze uncannily lifted her out of her loneliness precisely because it belonged to a creature that, although fenced in, could roam and gallop across acres and acres. And Alice rather liked the fences, the old wooden kind with two beams, horizontal—like the horizon—unobtrusive and even comforting, because they told you where things began and ended, and yet made you feel that the great beyond was just part of home.

A blasting boombox jolted Alice back to Ocean Avenue, at the gateway to Belmar. How like her father to skip over Spring Lake. Alice pointed at a parking space that had just opened, but he stepped on the gas and said it was too late. He just wouldn't park there. While admitting it was pleasant, he had always hated Spring Lake, as it evoked impossible lives entrenched in perfect lawns and perfect homes and perfect money. Belmar was much better. The old town was peeling and rough, much like Hank's cottage (and face), and even had its corners that felt vaguely down-and-out, and so unlike the Spring Lake make-believe. Times were hard, and they were only going to get harder, Hank mused, morning after morning, over the paper and coffee. We'll all be out in the street with this administration. The subprime mortgage mess had rattled Hank, who was sensitive about the whole issue of home and family, and he was lost in imaginings about entire towns going under with foreclosure, leaving desperate people behind. "We're headed toward a fucking wasteland," he explained to Alice, who needed some educating about the political nightmare the country was living through. "In Belmar alone there are 12 foreclosures. Where are these people gonna go, I ask you?" *How did he know there were 12?* Alice wondered. *He doesn't even live in Belmar!*

"Well, how many—" Alice began. Hank cut her off, anticipating her question.

"14. There are 14 in Eatontown."

"How do you know this?" Alice blurted out instead of asking *why* he knew it.

"A little hobby of mine. I bet you didn't know that there are foreclosure sites on the Web where the homes are posted. It's shocking, I tell you."

"*What's* shocking, Dad?"

"Don't you get it? People are like vultures, Alice, flying down on some carcass of a house and picking it clean. I wonder what kind of ghosts are in those foreclosed homes... I wouldn't live in one of them. Out of respect," he responded intently and, having expressed his thought so clearly, even to himself, found a new sense of pride in his home, despite the peeling paint and rumble tumble of the weeds.

As if by magic, a car pulled out of a space as if just for them, and Hank instantly turned the wheel and glided in, completely satisfied with himself. The hour was ripe with a cloud-dappled sky. It was a gentler hour, too; the sun beat less hard and the wind was mild. Father and daughter wandered, rather than walked, down the boardwalk, tasting the salt in the air, chatting about all the damned tourists. After a stretch, they stepped off the boardwalk in silent accord and made their way onto the wet sand, leaving their shoes near the ladder. Alice stopped every now and then to admire a sandcastle built with particular elegance. She was awed by one child's creation that boasted shell shutters and a seaweed roof. Hank was more taken by the ones that were half-broken by the waves, like sandy shipwrecks, and pondered how long it would take before the ocean swallowed them whole. Was it a matter of hours or minutes?

Alice was utterly amazed by the day, by the fact of her just being there, on the beach, with her father, at which moment his step picked up ever so slightly. A faint rumbling, or restlessness, began to steal into his mood, Alice was sure of it, and she began to struggle, silently, to find a way to keep him there, with her, just a moment longer. Hank turned an awkward smile toward his daughter and suggested that they head back to the car, and Alice responded hastily with a toss of her head in the opposite direction, toward the waves.

"Come on, let's go in! Before they die down!" Indeed, the roar of the surf had become tamer, and Hank too had noticed it, with disappointment, thinking he would check the tide table the next time he came to the shore.

"We have no towels! And it'll be dark soon, Alice." Hank began to turn back toward the boardwalk.

"No, Daddy, wait! Just a dip. Who cares?" she pleaded. And with that, she bounded into the ocean and dove into the body of what looked like the last huge wave of the day, just before it broke. She came up laughing like a rebellious mermaid, and Hank, persuaded, dove in after her.

The sun was now languid, and Hank, growing more anxious with the coming of dusk, coaxed Alice out of the water. His frustration grew with their failure to find their shoes, and Alice could hear him cussing under his breath. "Oh fuck it," he retorted to no one in particular, and they got into the car and backed out barefoot. Strangely enough, Hank began to sweat while his daughter, chilled, asked if they could put on the heat. "Of course, honey," he answered absently, and Alice was grateful for the endearment, although he said it so absently, in the throes of some sudden preoccupation.

The car sped up as if he were in a hurry for more than dry clothes. They got home just as evening thickened into dusk—but which glowed, eerily, in the light of the rising moon—and Hank found himself walking Alice to her car and urging her to get going, despite her soaking clothes and sand-covered limbs. The idea of her coming in for a shower and a change (he surely had a pair of shorts and a T-shirt that would do the trick, at least until she got back to Jenna's) didn't even occur to him. In fact, he suddenly seemed just to want his daughter to pull away and drive off into the night so he could run inside and hide. Disconcerted, but responding to his mood, Alice got into the car and backed out of the driveway, feeling the coarse tingle of her father's nightly beard that had scraped her cheek as he gruffly said goodbye.

Wet and sticky with ocean brine, an uncomfortable bare foot on the pedal, and fearful of the darkening sky, Alice found herself driving slowly just the same. It wasn't so much her father's rushing her away. She, too, had little desire to remain, preferring to clutch at whatever beauty there was to the day, however tinged by sadness. There she was, caught, or rather, suspended, on that road back to her mother's house, wheels gliding or hydroplaning, decidedly not gripping the ground. While her father's home would never be hers, she felt, at least, that she was very much his daughter after all. But the thought chilled her, despite its awkward coziness, as she turned into Jenna and Jason's driveway, as if the unsettled, oddly homeless feeling that was her father's, had, for altogether different reasons, now become her own. And she stepped into the house, haltingly, as her mother stared back at this stranger in the hallway, drenched and covered with sand.

II. Adam

It's strange how fears come and go, Adam thought as he woke up with the kind of yawn you make, not when you're tired but with the satisfaction of a good night's sleep, which he also thought was strange. Why yawn at all if you're not tired? He set aside that second question for now, imagining his father would have the answer since *he* always yawned—loudly even—when *he* woke up but continued to ponder fear. How could he be *so scared* that for days he was scared all the time, and then found himself now just looking out the window, watching the trees move quietly in the wind? It was true that his father could make sense of things in a matter-of-fact kind of way, and so simply that he could easily repeat it back to himself at a moment's notice:

> "There are two kinds of werewolves," Daddy said, "the ones who *choose* to shape-shift and the ones that *can't help it*, like Lupin on that full moon night."

This helped Adam consider the problem in a different way; and as time went on, it had the ambiguous effect of making him feel sympathy for Lupin—it wasn't his fault!—while also making him afraid someone might—on purpose—burst into another skin without warning. After all, some kids could just turn on each other unexpectedly, as he'd seen in the schoolyard. In a separate conversation, Mama told him that the werewolf came out of someone else's imagination. This had the important visual effect for Adam of watching the wolf hunch over and exit his mind and go back to that other person's head, which was even a little funny. But most of all, it was Adam himself and his confident strut, back and forth, on the wooden terrace overlooking the ocean, that drove the werewolf from the Cove. Yes, his armor had made

104

all the difference, and he was so proud when he wore it. And yet, he sometimes felt the werewolf's presence, remotely, when he went unprotected on hikes, at the beach, in the bath. But he kept that to himself, worried that words could bring it back again; so he would whisper about it to the fairies—the tooth fairy had invited her friends from Acadia— who agreed to protect the Cove at all times, day *and* night, just in case.

Having thought it through, and feeling better about it, he pulled open another set of curtains to let more light into the shaded room and coax his parents into starting the day. Set in the back of the house, the room upstairs, where they all slept, was the only one that didn't face east, and was further protected by fir tops that clung to the air with a sappy scent. Still early, the morning light was gentle enough to wash over Luke without waking him. Emma, on the other hand, loved this time of day most of all and would always get up the earliest. She'd in fact been awake all along, watching Adam look out at the day and was relieved for him that he could relax again and look out the window without fear. She met his eager face with a silent nod, not wanting to wake Luke, and joined her son in the anticipation of the day that lay before them—the last, in fact, of that vacation.

"You go first, Mama, and I'll follow," Adam insisted at the top of the darkened staircase that always jarred him with uncertainty. Fear had an architecture of its own, the way the stairs angled down to the bottom floor, for example, and the way the light from the kitchen rose ghost-like toward the top of the steps. Emma's mind met his and understood his hesitation, so why insist and push him toward it? She also liked being the leader and was in a rush, always, to lay eyes on the cove waters lunging out to meet the Atlantic Ocean. Her gaze would fill with that silver-blue light that had only the horizon as a vanishing point, and she would disappear along with it into endless space. Returning to herself, she was moved by the undercurrents and all that crustaceous life growing limitless beneath them, like the crazy lobster the fisherman bragged about, a 40-pounder, decades old. That lobster must have molted fifty times or more, swollen with change, cracking out of its shell, hideously vulnerable each time it shed, hiding for weeks in the darkest nook of the rocky floor, hidden in the shadows till its outer core hardened again, silent and still, beyond the reaches of the diving birds that plunged their beaks below the surface and broke out victorious with the morning's catch.

Adam followed the fluttering nightgown downstairs and was braced by the awkward chill of the Maine morning. Emma threw on a big wooly sweater and hurried Adam onto the couch, blanketing him in and setting a stack of books beside him. But he preferred to look out with her onto the wide view of the Cove; the whole wall of the living room was paned, so they could see it all, the soft blue sky and an ocean of wet shadows, the birds that raced across the beach, the rocky cliffs that lined the shore, and the small islands dotting the water with bright green, the whitish tide rushing up around them. His mother perched on the sofa's edge while they watched the fishing boats purr into the Cove to gather their nets and traps—"pretend traps," Adam called them, since they let lobsters scramble out for the most part (and thank God for that, he sighed when he heard about it). The day was so clear that Adam was sure he could see the claws of a captured lobster clipping at empty air, scuttling hopelessly on the fishy deck, and heard, or so he thought, a fisherman yelling to a friend to calm the thing down. What a relief that it outsmarted those windblown men and escaped back into the water, at least in his mind's eye. He remembered then that it was the fishermen's job to catch them and, not knowing how to reconcile those two facts, decided to drop them in favor of something else that had been on his mind.

"Why do boys' voices get lower and girls' get higher?" he inquired. Emma never answered right away, which was always a little frustrating, though he knew she was thinking carefully about it. Still, he cleared his throat to hurry her along.

"Girls' voices don't actually get higher—it just seems that way in contrast—but boys' voices do get lower. Come to think of it, girls' voices also get a little lower, but not as much as boys'. There are changes that happen in the body when kids get older, and that's one of them."

"But why do their voices *get* lower? Is there something in their throat?" He cleared his own again to feel it functioning as usual. He didn't like that something was going to happen inside him that he couldn't control.

"It has to do with hormones, which are natural and inside all of us," she explained. "Hormones are our life force; they tell the body what to do as it grows up."

"Okay, but what I want to know is, why do voices get *lower*. What do the hormones do to make it *sound* that way?" Just then, Luke came into the room, greeting them with his own deep, groggy voice.

"Like that, Mama. Like Daddy's voice. You hear what I mean? What'll happen to *my* voice when *I'm* a teenager? Where will it go? Will I be the same person?"

"You will always be you, Adam. Some things are permanent. But as you grow, your voice box grows, too, and your vocal cords get longer and thicker, and that changes the sound of the vibration, it's what will make the voice sound lower." Adam swallowed intently as he imagined his cords getting long and thick, and coughed with mild horror. It was useful, though, having a scientific explanation. He'd sat with his mother at the library many times, reading books about all the parts of the body, so this kind of talk was familiar to him.

"Come here, Adam, let me show you something," called his father, who had a large bird book in his hands and was flipping through the bright plates. "Look at these Purple Martins. This one's a male, and this one's a female. You see the difference?"

"Yes, the male is dark purple, and the female is brown... Hey, it's the same with all the birds," Adam noted as Luke turned the pages. "It doesn't seem fair, does it, Mama?" he asked, afraid that she would feel bad about not having all those colors since she was a female, too.

"It's okay. I think the females are brown so they can blend in with the trees and bushes to protect their eggs. That's how nature looks after the animals. It's called "camouflage". It's nice to have a secret and disappear without actually having to go somewhere to hide."

"Yes, I know about camouflage, but is the male bird's voice *lower* than the female's?" He clearly wasn't satisfied with Emma's answer to his question.

"Well, they sing to each other," his father replied, "calling back and forth, especially when they're happy."

"Yes, but is the male's voice *lower*?"

"Uh, I think they sing differently," Luke continued. "The longer songs are mostly male. Females call rather than sing. At least I think that's right.

"And some females don't sing at all, and most pelicans are silent," his mother added. At this, Adam jumped up and almost yelled, "But you said that's what happens when boys grow up!"

Luke felt somewhat unsure of himself when it came to these sorts of discussions, unlike Emma, who loved to study nature. She could name the trees in Acadia by looking at their leaves—even the pines, by glancing at their needles and cones. For all that he argued in favor of remaining grounded in reality when watching a play or film, especially when it was disturbing, Luke was more comfortable standing on the side of fiction when it came to the *why* of reality and its strange ways. Fiction offered explanations that were more accessible to him since he dwelled so often there, and drew on it metaphorically in his explanations to Adam about the world.

"So when Lupin turned into a werewolf, was that his way of growing up? Or did he stop being a human? Or did he stop being a male?" asked Adam, eager to examine the question from these other angles.

"He was a male the whole time, but at that moment, he was an animal. After the full moon, he became human again. Anyway, Adam, as we said, there's no such thing as werewolves," his father replied, careful to keep that beast at bay.

"But the ones in peoples' imagination howl, so how do you know if the howling is from a male or a female?"

"Uh—"

"So if Lupin turned into a werewolf, he might have turned into a *female* werewolf. You just can't tell from the voice," Adam confidently said. "I wish I could be a bird. Their voices don't get lower," he went on, saddened at the idea of losing his voice. "But I guess if I didn't get a lower voice, I wouldn't be able to use a lightsaber," he added sagely.

"A lightsaber? Oh, you mean like Luke Skywalker," said Emma. "I guess it's true that none of the women in *Star Wars* use a lightsaber, though Princess Leia does use a gun."

"Guns aren't anywhere near as cool as lightsabers, Mom."

"Yeah, but my question is this. Can only a man be a Jedi and use a lightsaber?" Emma asked, much as Adam would.

"*No*, Mom, Leia is Luke Skywalker's twin sister, and she has powers, too. 'The force runs strong in my family,'" said Adam, mimicking Luke Skywalker. "Anybody in the galaxy can be a Jedi, including Leia if she trains to be a knight." He looked longingly at his knight costume out on the porch, headed out to play, the conversation over. Then, at the door, he turned back and said, "Hey, Dad, your name is *Luke*. Are you a Jedi?"

"Well, is the world a movie?" his father asked, much as Adam would.

"It's *like* a movie," Adam replied. "Good and bad things happen. Anyway, movies *feel* real. I mean, what happens in them feels real. And a movie *is* a real thing, right?" And without further ado, he went out to the terrace and donned his armor, grabbed his sword, and flew off to fight the enemy beneath the trees, now totally uninterested in growing up, yet sensing, uneasily, that he wouldn't have much choice in the matter.

It was their last day in Maine, and Adam was relieved. He was exhausted from the whole ordeal, although he loved his armor, in which he fought many winning battles, and especially the magic sword that protected him at night. In fact, if someone—like Alice, who knew he had been scared—asked him about his vacation in a serious kind of way, he might even say it had all been worth it, except that he really would much rather live in a world without werewolves. He turned his attention back to his parents, who were asking him what he'd like to do, some special thing, Mama said. Hiking up Beech Mountain one last time was the obvious choice, whose fire tower, perched incongruously on the summit like an odd pagoda, delighted him more than any peak in Acadia.

Up they climbed, awed by the diving views of Long Pond. As they wound their way to the top, they stopped to gather—could it be true?—huckleberries. *Huckleberries!* Adam could hardly believe a fruit had a name like that! It sounded exotic in ways that backwoods, streams and fields always did to this city kid who rediscovered them in their endless possibilities of bugs and worms and toads, kneeling to play in the fragrant winds till his legs were chaffed. He had never encountered any food that sounded like *huckle*; it *had* to come from those woods! It sounded suspiciously like *chuckle* (was it a joke?), and that you could only find on a trail. Its sour taste made the fruit all too real and was just as surprising as its name—so unlike the wild blueberry growing in handfuls everywhere, and so sweet it seemed like the fruit of a fairytale. Years later, in middle school, he was jolted into recollection of Beech Mountain when the teacher assigned *Huckleberry Finn*. Adam understood why that brave boy preferred to be called "Huck"—no *Huckleberry* could ever go down the Mississippi on a raft with a runaway slave. His teacher had trouble following his train of thought, but then, it was a rare teacher who could. It all made sense when he considered that huckleberries only grew wild. So he was especially eager to pick them during that climb up Beech Mountain, knowing he wouldn't find them back in the city. Adam peered into every possible bush to harvest them for his mother, who rejoiced every time he opened his sweaty hand to show a berry or two. She sure could get excited about little things, thought Adam, as he hurried to keep up with Luke's brisk step while Emma dreamed about the peaks that she would climb next summer. Adam felt her sadness hanging over the mountain, and imagined pushing it back into the woods so she'd feel better. He chattered away to keep her cheerful, running to and fro, hands alternately full then empty of berries, and grinned at the thought of his return to the city and his beloved Alice. He wondered if she would dare eat a huckleberry, and he put one in his pocket to surprise her.

As Emma looked out at the world from atop Beech Mountain, Echo Lake seemed strangely transformed with its steel-gray surface, as if devoid of depth, shroud-like and eerie, when a sudden gust blew clouds across its surface reviving its ripples until the fluffy cluster, having sped across the breadth of the Lake, crashed onto the beach and disappeared. Off to the north, the Harbors boasted continual activity and, just beyond, the Cranberry Islands sat contentedly at the mouth of the ocean, ripe and green. Usually, at such moments, Emma would get restless with hiking fever. She would have to coax—or bribe—Adam into leaving his throne up on the fire tower, then detach Luke from the boulder that he had melded into, deep in meditation, so they could resume their journey. But on that last day of vacation, it was she who was having trouble coming off the peak despite Luke's restlessness (in his mind, he was already at his desk, working away at his new drama) and Adam's glad anticipation (he was already in his room, at play, with Alice). She felt them gone, back in the city, while she just couldn't take another step, and struggled to keep them with her in that world of crests and depths.

"Why don't we go down the mountain another way?" she suggested, heading toward the cliff and the dimly drawn trails that dropped down from at least two different angles. Adam was wary of the unfamiliar path, and Luke didn't even try to hide his irritation; they did have to pack, after all. But she went dipping down despite their yelled objections, with no idea where they were going but confident that hiking down this unknown trail was well deserved. Why shouldn't they have one last adventure? And her certainty ballooned into a sort of giddiness. Besides, they'd find themselves at the foot of the mountain in no time since it took just under an hour to climb up here. As she turned back toward them with a searching smile, Adam quickened his step without question, while Luke, bringing up the rear, cussed under his breath. Nevertheless, he was soon marveling aloud at the piney wonders of the forest while Emma strode ahead with quickened heart.

The sun was a paler ball of yellow at that late afternoon hour, then disappeared from sight as the trail wound deeper into the woods. Curiously, they had seen no hikers for the past half hour. Adam pointed out that it was getting dark, and Emma—despite her growing uneasiness at the uncommon thickness of trees and vines—reassured him that the sky was as bright as ever, though they couldn't see it. Clearly they were descending, although less steeply. But reconsidering the trail, she realized they probably had left Beech Mountain and now were wandering along a cliffside that was stonier, more slippery with moss, and without a signpost in sight. In fact, the trail was often vanishing into the forest floor, under the thick cover of leaves and branches. Emma ran ahead to find it again, then motioned them to follow.

"You really don't know where we are, do you, Mama?" Adam asked quietly.

She went along pretending that she knew exactly what she was doing: "We're in Cathedral Woods"—the first place that came to mind—but which was in fact on Monhegan Island, off the coast of Boothbay Harbor, over 100 miles away. Well, it was in Maine, anyway, and naming it gave her a semblance of authority. She had walked through those woods as a child with her friend Jackie, bringing cookies to the fairies where their houses clustered in patches of emerald moss roofs held up by small stout branches, and the floors were tiled blue with muscle shells. The fragrance was intoxicating, the same mingling of citrus and grassy pine that imbued whatever mountain they were on now; the same spruce and balsam firs crowned above them with piney arches, a green cathedral gilded with light brown cones that bowed in clusters, while others, purplish-green, stood upright on delicate branches. The memory brought her back there to Cathedral Woods when she was Adam's age; she trembled with the sense of timelessness.

"Cathedral Woods? What's that?"

"A magical place with a secret for some lucky few."

"It is? Tell me!"

"I'll have to whisper it to you," Emma said, drawing him close to cup her hand around his ear. Adam stood grinning as he learned that little fairies lived there in a whole world of their own, hidden from humans. Watching Emma and Adam locked in fairy talk irked Luke. He didn't see the point of devising such stories, especially when Adam had struggled so much with the Potter film. Besides, their priority was getting off the mountain and back to the car. Seeing the lines deepen in his wife's brow, he dropped the criticism for the moment and stood by, sensing nervousness in her elation. Their eyes met, and Emma knew instantly what he was thinking. From her point of view, there was nothing wrong with magical thinking, especially if it could help children feel powerful. While she no longer believed in fairies, she remained attuned to a kind of hidden life, or a presence, that emanated from objects or that infused the atmosphere; things seemed to brim more thickly for her, or made her quiver with this secreted tinge of another life form. She felt it especially when she drew and searched for it in her drawings.

Some years later, however, when Adam was around 10, he went to her quite broken up about all these things they called magic. This was not real, he told her—or was it, clinging to a last doubt. Were they stories she had told him pretending they were true? His mother had to admit that he was right and sunk heavily with remorse about fairies and the way the mountains of Maine bequeathed gems to lucky children, gems she had planted herself down the trails for Adam to discover. He listened quietly. Well, he didn't regret those stories because they were fun. Besides, even if those things weren't real, he told her, that didn't mean that magic didn't exist. It was a feeling, not a fact. But for years, Emma wondered what those stories meant, why she told them to Adam, and if it had all been a mistake. She finally settled on the idea that stories—the ones she invented or the ones she passed down—gave Adam a way of weaving together impressions into something coherent. But it was also possible that they made it harder for him to grow up. Emma felt the child within herself peering out onto the world, and her teenage self still throbbing in her skin. This was part of the reason she liked being a mother; she could be these younger selves that had not gone away. She remembered the superheroes that broke out of their Playdough skin the summer before. Perhaps his donning the knight's costume was reminiscent of the surprise life beneath the outer bearings.

"But how do you *know*, Mama?" Adam said, doubting that fairies really did live in the woods. How could they be all over the place, out at the Cove with him, and now here? The darkening forest was a reality, and she could see how it gnawed at the secret world she was trying to create. But she felt the need to engage him in the woods rather than let fear encroach upon him.

"Just look around you! There's moss everywhere!"

Adam had no idea what she was talking about, but welcomed the distraction from the strange dark trail, his heart nevertheless at a quickened pace which made his hands sweaty. "What you mean by the moss, Mama!"

"That's what the fairies use to build their houses. Come look how soft and green it is!" Adam crouched against a moss-covered boulder and rubbed his cheek and hands against it, confirming his mother's description, although it was a little damp, and he didn't like the wet patches on his knees much. "But do the fairies live inside the moss? Where are their houses?"

"Well, we actually need to help build them. Here, you see this bit of turned-up moss? Get some twigs and leaves and bring them to me," she commanded, avoiding Luke's gaze. Adam was back within moments, and they set about making a few fairy shelters at the foot of a pine that was slightly uprooted, then stood up to admire their work. "People don't realize that fairies live here," she continued, "so we have to be very careful and protect them." Adam rose, then gently jumped off the boulder he was perched on so as not to disturb his new friends. After all, the tooth fairy said that children could see fairies, even if their parents couldn't, and Adam imagined that the fairies could therefore see him, and he didn't want to scare them away.

As much as Luke understood the necessity of distracting Adam, it was going on much too long. "Would you all mind very much leaving the fairies behind so we can go home and pack? Where are we anyway, Emma?" They had left the map at home, certain they wouldn't need it as they had climbed Beech Mountain so many times. They had no way of situating themselves.

Now the sun was setting, and the look on Emma's face confirmed Luke's fear that they were actually lost. Adam saw something that looked like fear in his father's face—a look he'd never seen before. He turned to his mother for reassurance and wondered why she looked away. The pine began to crackle more loudly under their feet and the cliffs seemed to fall away into darkness. Emma took her child's hand and led them deeper down the trail.

"Mama, I'm scared," Adam whispered, trying not to cry.

"Don't worry, honey, it's okay, I promise." Then she opened her hand for Adam as if she were offering a wonderful gift.

"What is it, Mama?"

"Why, Adam, I was counting on you! Only you can see her!"

Well, it was better to be a child after all, it seemed. Adam took his mother's cue and acknowledged aloud the presence of the little fairy who glowed in her hand like a firefly.

"Fairy, lead us down the mountain!" Emma ordered, gently blowing the fairy off her hand. "You see? All we have to do is follow her!"

Luke thought better of interfering with this flight of fancy, but kept looking on the sly for other hikers who could help them out of this mess, while Emma and Adam tripped more confidently down the trail—sometimes truly tripping, as Adam pointed, from tree to rock to bush, at the fairy that his mother couldn't see. Adam marveled at how lucky they were that the fairies also lived in this part of the woods; but as they left behind the mossy terrain, he worried that the fairy would abandon them, or get lost without the emerald green floor to guide her. Emma reassured him that the fairy knew all the mountains of Acadia like the back of her hand, and sometimes only came home to sleep with her family after a full day of exploring. Besides, she had her beam of light to help her see.

"But she's only a child! How can she go out without her parents?"

"It's different for fairies. They're very clever and can take care of themselves. They can dart out of the way of a mountain lion in the wink of an eye!"

"*A mountain lion?* Are there *mountain lions* here, Daddy?" Luke, doing his best to hide his irritation, turned to Emma, who was sure to have the answer.

"They used to live here, like the grey wolves, but they're all gone now," she said, realizing all too quickly that she'd only made things worse.

"Grey *wolves?* Maybe there's still one left who didn't escape!" Could there be a *werewolf* in the woods? Adam's mouth went dry as he tried to peer through the treetops at the moon, but it hadn't risen yet. He turned to his father who picked him up and held him close, so he wouldn't lose his footing in the twilight.

Soon the path veered off abruptly, and they found themselves peering over the edge of a cliff at the silvery sheen below. It was Echo Lake, Emma said, from a more southern angle. The sky was now pale grey with light pink clouds that carried the last light of the day. They guessed they were somewhere near Beech Mountain and pushed ahead; but the trail began to hug the cliff until it was only a mere ledge, with room enough for single file. Luke set the child down in front of him. Adam wondered how his parents could have led him to such a place where one of them might fall off the mountain. For the first time in his life, a terrible suspicion entered his mind: his parents actually didn't know as much as they said they did.

"Adam, don't look down!" Emma commanded in a strong voice, seeing the trail pick up a little further ahead and that safety was in reach. "Do not take your eyes off my back! Daddy is right behind you, and I'm in front, and we will be fine." Adam obeyed and soon found himself on broader ground. He looked up at his mother whose face was glowing with sweat, her eyes shining back at him. She hugged him quickly so he wouldn't notice her relief, but he knew full well that she was just as scared as he was, despite her voice sounding in charge, and he took her hand to comfort her. Emma, gazing back at the steep drop, finally understood they had wandered onto Beech Cliff. And while the trail had brought them to the edge for a terrifying moment, it soon wove gently down the mountain, away from the cliff.

"Look, Mama, the fairy is back! She'll show us the rest of the way!"

They were finally heading off the mountain; a wooden arrow planted in the earth pointed toward "Parking", where they would soon find their red car that would take them back to Bar Harbor. Bog walks led them off the end of the muddy trail, and Adam, feeling wistful though exhausted, made it his business to gather a last bundle of magic wands that he begged to take back to the city. Emma agreed, despite the rule that she felt guilty for breaking, even at that late hour, that hikers take nothing away from Acadia. Adam reluctantly said goodbye to the fairy who had saved his life and wondered if he would ever see her again. He felt a shadowy sort of sadness as he sat in the car while his dad reached for the keys and placed them in the ignition. He looked out the window at the dark woods. He would return to her, she would surely be there, waiting for him, next summer. Fairies never left Acadia, Mama had explained, and Adam wondered if it was because of the moss or if everyone, including fairies, needed to stay close to home. He thought fondly of his room in the city with the pile of leaves in the corner where he would put his magic wands, and thought that at the very least, he could keep a little of the mountain with him. As his father pulled out of the parking lot, Adam waved good-bye one last time to his friend. He had come down from Beech Mountain uncertain. Without her little beam of light, how would he find his way?

III. Emma

Emma raised the quarts of wild blueberries from their protective embrace of socks, towels, and T-shirts, carefully packed lest they meet a crushing fate at the airport due to careless hands. Hands were everything, and Emma had sighed in resignation when those first palms heaved the forest-green bag onto the TSA conveyor belt. The taut vinyl shell was likely no match for the next set of hands, bin-throwing this time, which threw it into the cart with utter disregard for the precious cargo of berries deep within; down but not out, the unsteady bag would meet its third heavily-knuckled pair, poised to heave and ram it haphazardly into the plane's lower holds. Huddled together, all that flight's luggage would then suffer the indignities of turbulence and screeching engines until welcomed on the hot tarmac by other sets of hoisting, heaving clutches.

What did it matter? It would all be jam in the end. But when it came to mountain memory and jam making, such things did matter to Emma, who looked forward to the moment when she would hover over the magically real kitchen counter where hard culinary science meets the poetry of scent and hue. She would've gotten right down to it the night before, the moment she crossed the threshold, if she weren't so exhausted from the trip home. She was content to just sit with Blacky, who whined loudly about her absence, visibly transformed, having shed a few pounds while they were all away, despite the lovely cat sitter keeping him company. Now, in the early morning hours, the house sat heavily in the summer stillness, ceding to the murmur of her steps. Would he keep her company till the last jar was wiped clean of sticky drippings? She warned the cat that it would take hours; she had a good 30 mason jars to fill. She met his gaze and eased herself into his purring forgiveness.

She had felt such remorse about leaving him! While he was finally glad to see her, she wished that she were half as glad to be back home.

But first to the Green Market, as the desire to sketch and draw was just as pressing. She had thought long and hard about the unlikely pairing on paper of blackberry clusters with some dirt-filled bunches of radishes. The reverie was compelling in its precision—it had to be blackberries, and it had to be radishes. It would express her growing preoccupation with life occurring in underground and over-ground space—the visible and the internal—and the cross-section of those worlds. Unearthed radishes pulsated with bulging dark-pink bulbs, their exposed white tentacles reaching out into the air for the earth that once hid them and where they would be roots. Emma was interested in the round variety and its strange likeness to an image she'd once seen of fat-storing cells surrounded by connective tissue. The closeness was almost too close, as if inner—and microscopic—life were now exposed in the vegetable, the connective tissue and web of roots one and the same, the one buried in tissue, the other in moist garden dirt. As for the blackberries, she was drawn to how they trailed the ground but belonged to the bramble in the air, their cell-like druplets shining like beads of black onyx, a wild mineral fruit clinging tight to its stem, clustering around a hidden and small white ovary. And she was struck by how they'd bleed when over-ripe or when the skin wall was pierced, whereas the radish was as white and as unoozing as stone. For all its precision, the reverie was not a visualization of the drawing to come. It was preparatory in the way that it presented possibilities of pulled-out life, but she knew not what the drawing would actually look like, nor what the juxtaposition of radishes and blackberries would actually yield. Black and deep pink were now absolutely right; tentacles and druplets, earth, leaf, pulp and air were imperative.

She could hear the din from blocks away, but it was far worse in the hot Square itself, angry with street noise and exhaust and packed with tourists. Emma grabbed some radishes and a few boxes of berries and hurried her step back down University Place, shielding herself as best she could from the oppressive city. She was certain, nevertheless, that wandering on its fringes would be far worse than the place itself. She could not bear disconnection, but that morning she was bereft, and uncertain of how to return to that city which had always held out so much possibility to her.

Adam greeted her at the door, bouncing with questions as she wearily set down her basket. There were no flowers in her arms, which was unusual for his mother, who always came back from the market with bright colored blooms. He felt the sadness and noticed her mouth tugging downwards. He tried not to let it spoil his joy at seeing Alice, and could Mama call her that very minute since Alice had promised to come over *right away*? Had this happened even an hour later, Emma would have taken Adam by the hand, sweaty with excitement, and called Alice with shared anticipation. But now, raw and unrooted, she needed a moment to pull herself together. She thought to turn to Luke for comfort, but he was already behind closed doors, deep in thought about *Skyline*. Like Emma and Adam, he wasted no time plummeting headfirst into the things that mattered most. Steadying herself with a look at the sky and glancing at the plants on the terrace—they had more or less survived the scorching heat—she turned back with more courage to her child's impatient gaze. It was still early; would they wake her? Little did she know that Alice had been up since before dawn, awaiting the call so she could come see her little friend again.

Adam sat in the hallway, outside the apartment door, on the wooden chair that he'd dragged out there the moment

Emma confirmed that Alice would come over just as soon as she got dressed. Despite Emma's appeals to reason—Alice wouldn't arrive for at least another hour—Adam sat with his eyes fixed straight down the hallway, not wanting to miss the moment she stepped out of the elevator. Emma, now at work on her jam, was soon preoccupied with the blueberries, which had survived the trip home without a trace of damage, and seemed an even deeper hue of purple-blue than they had up on the mountain, nesting amid the glossy egg-shaped leaves protecting the tiny fruit. She rinsed and dried them by the thousands, and the countertop was soon covered with deep dots, some bleeding slightly on the paper toweling where they lay. Blacky watched from his perch atop the refrigerator, uncertain as to where he could jump down when he got hungry. Everyone in (or just outside) the house was engrossed in something or other in utter silence, except when Adam would cross the universe and poke his head into the kitchen to ask the time and if Alice would be there soon. Sighing for the umpteenth time, he trudged back to his station and devised a ditty about waiting all day.

As he rose again, minutes later, about to kick his chair over in frustration, he found himself in mid-air instead, startled by the electric sound of the buzzer. Would Mama come to the elevator right away with him? This was daunting, as Emma was about to set a boiling jar on a wooden board and didn't want to break away from her preserves. Couldn't he run down to greet Alice on his own? Caught between kitchen and hallway, Emma finally bent towards Adam, who was dancing around and chanting the floor number that he imagined Alice was on as she rose to the 16th floor on the elevator. He would simply not forgive her if they were not there together to scream *hello* as the doors opened on Alice's beaming face. Their embrace lasted what seemed like ten minutes. Emma finally walked back down the hall, turning around as she reached the doorway and calling out that she would meet them back inside, but wasn't sure they'd even heard her.

The radishes sat limp and dirty on her worktable. The heat and car exhaust had drained them of all signs of life. To perceive a thing that way at 3:00 in the morning was unusual for Emma. In fact, it had never happened. At that hour, when the world was asleep, everything—from the faint screech of her chair as she set it in position, to the newspaper lying on the coffee table, even the refrigerator, dull in its rectangular utility—came uncannily forward, filling the air with the tension of a customary thing betrayed by her awareness, uprooting the object from its usual purpose. The tension in that sneaker tipped on its side became almost palpable; the monotony of the refrigerator hum vaguely threatened her with impending... what? The Revenge of the Appliance overheated for the last time to serve the human race... Emma could not exactly name what happened in the room in those deep hours of the night, but what she did know was that the vegetables strewn on her table would become increasingly more animate. It had taken her years to develop a relationship with her pencil, a separate entity that was nevertheless an extra digit, the first and foremost into which the others would impart shifts of pressure and mood. And there was the fact that she had never had rigorous studio training. She would never know if that was for the better or worse. But she was after more than craft, more than re-creation of a thing; it was about catching its animate quality and setting it free again to settle in the textured paper, then re-emerge amid the shadows.

Was it the atmosphere, or was it the pencil itself that brought this tension into the foreground? Some years back, her eyes fixed on the pencil she had picked up to draw some vegetable, it came to her that there was something predetermined in its mixture of clay with graphite: drawing was like sculpting, sculpting light as it hit an object. The world around her became so vivid that objects began to drift, ever so slightly, veering off somewhere, toward a twilight state, not from within but from without, from the carrots themselves, the radishes or the peppers themselves. The distinction was essential and had everything to do with both the process and the drawing, which was *not*, decidedly, anthropomorphic. The vegetables just seemed to exist intensely in that room at 3:00 a.m., and she tried to render it on paper.

But that night, the radishes sat limp and dirty. To say they were *dirty* did justice to the problem, for Emma had a thing about dirt—loved it, both the texture and the smell, and was keenly aware of how it roused the root vegetables into their link with the earth. But there was nothing nascent about these radishes that she grabbed in haste that morning from the market; the dirt was a dusty dirty, which irritated Emma, whose mood lowered as the night wore on. She could sit with those radishes till dawn, and nothing would happen. The same with the berries, despite the victory at finding a quart still attached to their stems. Her hands fell into her lap. She bent her head down and observed them as if they were detached from herself. The index finger of her right hand caught her eye; she studied it attentively, unable for a moment to completely recognize it as her own. This was due not to her state of mind, but to the bend that started at the middle knuckle, sending the rest of the finger off on a slight angle to the right. It actually looked *crooked*. Emma was taken aback by this discovery, and wondered why it was that she had never noticed it before. It was probably the first sign of arthritis. A flash of her grandmother's hands, knotted and gnarly, gave her a start. While she was tempted to be done with it and call it a night, she continued gazing at that hand until she reached for a pencil with her left, her gesture briefly breaking the stillness of the moment. There she sat, deeply engrossed for the next few hours, drawing her own crooked index finger. Her hand rested on its side on the table, allowing her to reflect the tension in the finger that was pointing, vaguely, somewhere, nowhere. Every muscle of her body tensed up over this problem. The activity disoriented her somewhat; she never drew the human body, not since her teenage years when she went to life drawing classes. But the dim metamorphosis of age that had transformed her own bone and skin was, at that moment, more compelling than the farmer's choicest root vegetable, freshly harvested.

The sound of light footsteps and chair legs dragging jolted her from her state of concentration. There was Adam a few feet away from her, half-dressed and looking for something. He didn't say anything to her—in fact, he didn't even see her, which was unlike the child who always called out for her when he woke up in the middle of the night. Emma called to him gently, but he didn't answer. He must be sleepwalking, she realized. He looked lost there, searching for a thing not of this world. She quietly guided him by the shoulders back into his room. She laid him down in his bed and, feeling the weight of exhaustion, stretched out alongside him. Sensing her there, he whispered: "Let's hold each other and float in space together."

She got up and walked over to the mirror. As her reflection looked back at her, a third eye opened in her forehead, over her left eye, looking back at her, unmistakably. It was a darker shade of brown than her own, richer, deeper; it felt like it could be her eye, but wasn't. It was of her, and it wasn't. It was her gaze but extended from something else. Overcome and slightly sickened, she began to fall, slowly, then faster, as if she were rushing away, until she hit consciousness when she sat up with a start.

Adam was still sleeping next to her. He never slept past 7:00, and here it was 9:45. That alone was almost more astounding than the dream—so vivid and somehow true, that she ran into the bathroom to see if that third eye was really there. So she was not a freak; and yet she had the strangest feeling that the eye *was* there, just beneath the surface of her brow, ready to open at some mysterious moment. Why now? Nothing came to her. She slid back down under the blanket next to Adam, who sensed her presence and woke up. It had always been this way: for the first six months of Adam's life, he slept little more than six hours a day and never all at once. Life was just too exciting for the infant who didn't want to miss a second of it. Things had not changed so much from those days, she mused, except for the essential difference that, when they came together, it seemed that they arrived from more separate worlds, which had something to do with the dream, whose eeriness was still at large. Meanwhile, Adam was asking what was for breakfast.

As she went into the kitchen and looked at the clock, Emma realized that they had seriously overslept. Amazingly, it was 10:30. She'd forgotten that this was his first day of science camp, where he'd go for the next few weeks until school started. Well, there was no way she could get him there till noon, and it hardly seemed worth it since he'd be off to a shaky start, getting there three hours late, and Adam wasn't one to tolerate new beginnings under any circumstances. As it was, when she took him there the next morning, he cried until Charlie showed up. She was the closest thing to a sister; he had known her practically since birth. She showed up in the same playgroup with her sitter just months after she was adopted from Hawaii. She'd always had that look of the tropics about her, bright flowers and big waves as if she kept these things no matter what. He loved her with his whole heart because they played the best games ever, and he could just be himself. He loved her name—a boy's name for a girl—and Charlie had this way of not insisting they be one or the other; they took turns pretending to be girl and boy superheroes or warriors, inventing characters all day long. Yes, Charlie was there yelling *Adam* as she hurried to his side. She saw that he was crying and comforted him. Soon she had him by the hand and led him toward the monkey bars, as Emma slipped out of Madison Park into the hum of the city.

She meant to go straight home to unpack (the only things she'd taken from the suitcase were the blueberries and her toothbrush) and tend to the thousand details of mail, phone calls, and putting the house in order. But she was soon making her way uptown, vaguely aware there was some purpose to the deviation. Besides, the streets in mid-August weren't so bad. She could actually walk down the sidewalk freely, unassaulted by the crowd. Few cars murmured past, and the air hung slightly with a lull that every now and then opened a silent space in the city clamor, only to be inter-rupted, moments later, by a hum, a buzz, then a honk, and the whole thing would start up again. But the lull remained with her that morning as she walked along the avenues; Emma walked on within a drift of images, attuned to the strange pull leading her away.

It wasn't like she'd have anything to discover on the Upper East Side. It was more the *heading up* that seemed to be the draw. She scaled Lexington Avenue as if heading up an Acadian incline. Was that what she was looking for? That tension in her thighs as she pushed up with a firm foot onto a boulder, boosting herself to the next height? The quality of the trees grown squat and wind-blown as she neared the summit? Or was it the way she felt lifted, mentally, poised in wandering, twisting and turning with the trail, her imaginings studded with nests, animal tracks, and low-lying berries that would appear like sudden treasures, beckoning her to drift beyond the trail? She could smell the pines, rich, almost smoky under the high sun.

Up she climbed for miles until she got to East 78th Street—where a certain scent plunged her back into the present. She would know that smell anywhere, her mouth watering in anticipation. Apricots, tangy and bold, throbbed intensely in the morning sunlight. A store clerk prudishly cranked out the awning that veiled them in shade. But even in the shadow there was something hot about them, something that made them even more appealing, their skin a crazy gold, as if it were glowing, the whole heap beaming like hundreds of fat fireflies, larger than life, suddenly realizing it was day and yet intent on lighting something up. Emma would not look away though she didn't quite know what to do with such a moment of sheer excess. It had grown decidedly hot, and the air sat heavily on anything it could find. She looked at her watch: it was only 9:30.

She veered west to Central Park, where a breeze slightly whirled. She wandered up the lawns that had somehow survived the usual August burn, and stretched out in the smell of freshly cut grass, remembering all the rolls down that very hill with Adam, who would scream with pleasure, and a dizzy apprehension, until they hit bottom. She would always rise, completely happy, grass-stained and dizzy herself. She wondered how many more rolls down that hill she would have with her son, now a camper and headed for first grade. Something had unhinged itself since that last trip to Acadia. Maybe it had to do with the fairy and the way Adam called her to him when he was scared, struggling to steal back to something soothing, but which was growing more and more ephemeral. More likely it was the real person of Alice, darting in and out of his dreams and waking hours during that long month away—that young, dark-haired woman who still killed herself laughing like a child, but who, in her older way, made him feel like all was right with the world. It was clear that Adam loved her dearly and that this friendship had created a shift within. Returning from Acadia, *going home* had taken on new meaning for him. There was more to the world, calling him beyond the apartment door, and he hungered to be in it. In truth, Adam was a little boy no longer, but a boy, and this made all the difference. Emma turned away, her gaze drifting toward the Boat House. She made her way there in heavy haste.

She decided to rent a rowboat and glide lazily across the lake. It was, after all, one of her favorite pastimes, whose charm lay in its solitude. She could tune out the bits of conversation breaking through the breeze and the splash up and down of the many oars sprinkling all around her, whisking families, couples, or friends to their own coveted spots—a flat boulder, a willow, a grassy patch where they would anchor for lunch. She seemed to be the only one who ever took a boat out alone. She never told Luke about it, as if she had some adulterous secret. It was a delight to be alone with her own body in that boat, oars in their sockets, carefully balanced on the rims of the boat, dripping with lake water, as she lay back in the wooden vessel, looking at the big sky and feeling warm, too warm, from the sun. A cloud covered the bright ball for a moment, and Emma watched as it hovered over her, a puffy partner, big with breeze. They floated together in water and sky until the cloud, suddenly caught by an unexpected wind, sailed off like a white balloon and vanished. The sky, bereft of clouds, deepened its hue and became still again. The sun began to burn her face and neck.

It was better in autumn, she thought, when the tourists were gone, the air had a chill to it, and the breeze, when it was up, would stay up.

It was nearing noon. She pulled her boat into the dock and looked back across the lawn where the Ramble awaited, inviting her into its shady hills that hugged the water's edge. A yellow-grey puffball darted about as it entered the woods, a hooded warbler, its violet eye looking out from a lemon-yellow face, peering beneath its ink-black hood that stretched down like sideburns to its thick little bib. The female always went about with much less of a hood, stealing her way into lower wetlands in the winter months. But this fellow, clearly at home here, knew his trees, gaily chirping *ta wit ta wit ta wit tee yo* as it fluttered eagerly into the sacred Hackberry—which pushed her thoughts to *hackleberry* and finally land on *huckleberry*. She smiled, pronouncing it out loud in the same low voice as Adam's when he tried out *huckleberry* for the first time, laughing as the word popped off his lips. Her hooded friend had ventured there prematurely, Emma reflected, since the berries that those small spirited birds fed on were still orangey-red and wouldn't be ripe purple for another month. It darted away as if aghast at its mistake, then cheerily sped away in search of a lovely fat fly that would do nicely for a snack.

Having lost sight of the warbler, Emma thought she would speed away herself as she looked across the forest floor, vivid with cans and cigarette butts, papers and bags. Had she come all that way for this? Surely she couldn't spend her time craning her head upwards to avoid looking at the trash. Trying her best to connect to the place, she recognized the sycamore, identified four species of oak, and gathered some leaves for later use. But the effort made her weary. The Ramble—the meandering woodland haven for migrant birds and romantic souls—was trodden to the core. Even the tumbling Gill, which wound its way through the Ramble (where Adam would play for hours), seemed just a dull trickle with little life below its surface, and she cursed the man-made scene that replaced the swamps of the 19th century, in what had been a bold attempt to create the illusion of nature in the wild. Perhaps it wasn't a total fiasco, she tried to tell herself. If the Park were no longer a place of wandering, what would she become? Through the trees she saw the Lake, sitting vaporous and grand, a dense haze rising from its surface, making its way from one shore to another like a cloud rolling out from a blast of dry ice. Her thoughts cooled with flashes of winter skaters gliding across the silvery expanse, surrounded by white snowy hills. Such were the winters of her childhood, crowned with boughs, heavy with snow. She would walk through the wonderland with her friend Jackie, marveling at the icicles and how they caught the sunlight. The girls would each break one off and lick it like sugar cane, and the cold chilled their lips bright red. Would such winters, thick and deep, ever come again?

Something broke her reverie with a chaotic whisk of wings. A bat! Was it actually... *silver*? Emma was just as confused as the little creature who, seeming to realize its plight, disappeared before she could be sure of what she'd seen: a silvery *shadow* of a bat, or a bat itself? Emma hurried out the north end of the Ramble, feeling the world somehow askew, what with birds confounding berry seasons and bats flying around in broad daylight.

She was in the North Meadow. Her stomach growled as she stopped to watch a baseball game. She bought a bottle of water and continued north, wondering just how high she could go and why it was she couldn't stop. Her sticky limbs began to ache. Just ahead, the Wildflower Meadow was ablaze with goldenrod; the tall grass waved in a welcome breeze, and Emma collapsed there in the midst of late summer scents and weirdly cool soil, but lingered only for a minute or so. She gazed north with irritated restlessness, which left her at the sight of the Ravine. She made her way over, relieved to see that few were wandering there that day, at the western edge of the pond. She left them behind, lost under the thick forest canopy, drawn by the gush of her favorite waterfall. She kneeled down by the Loch, her knees pressing into the dense floor of leaves. Contemplating her reflection, Emma noted proudly that her face was truly dirty. Her eager hands dipped in and out of her amused glance as she cupped the cool waters then spilled them over her face. She knew that she was truly alone from the stillness of the earth that gathered around her bare legs. With a mischievous smile, she quickly stripped and, shaded by the frothing waterfall, bathed in secret under the summer sky.

The morbid feeling of the city as a tomb dissolved in the Pool where her splashes broke like laughter. Up from one last dive, her hair got tangled with loose leaves; she left them there, offering no explanation to Luke, when later, she pulled them from her clumps of pondy hair, smiling at him with no malice, but with some trepidation at the corners of her mouth that left him wondering where she had been, and who she was.

Dripping from head to toe, she stepped into her dusty clothes, which instantly were soaked, with lines of earthy rain trickling down her thighs. So much for the bath! Emma didn't mind in the least, although it was a bit uncomfortable to walk through the Ravine with soaking socks and sloshing shorts. Just a few steps from the waterfall, she came upon an odd sort of clearing which captured her attention—her whole being, in fact, as she sensed something beyond Nature there:

something deeper, more mysterious, something more to do with Myth, unearthly, its unplanned circularity swelling the geography with the suggestion of a gathering place for curious creatures. As she quieted her steps, she became aware that the spot itself was breathing, as if always alive, ageless.

Emma's climb finally ended as she stole quietly toward the center of that rounded clearing beneath the canopy of branches, and there beheld a most majestic tree, widely lobed with creviced trunk, bulging here and there with warts; a gnarly oak, stunted with twists and turns. Its boughs gathered around itself in crooked embrace. It had a fierce beauty about it, the dark experience of a thousand seasons. The clearing was completely surrounded by oaks, contrasting starkly with the stretch of forest just nearby, where all kinds of trees blotted the sky. But here, there was just old oak. From the cluster arose a sweet water scent, sap no doubt, still coursing through its veins, at a snail's pace. Emma put out her hand to touch the trunk, then timidly dropped it at her side. Still she approached, nevertheless, then stopped again, somehow captured by the presence.

She studied the tree, which seemed alive with stories of half-men hiding within and fleeing a beast; a shoulder here, a knee there, bulging out of the trunk, trapped momentarily; a lost child seeking refuge; a wounded raccoon recovering in a crook; lichens traveling up a hollow highway; an angry satyr hunting down a maiden. The oak was altogether sphinx-like in its metamorphic depths. Emma bent to pick up a small twig that had lately fallen, due maybe to some careless bird pecking around for a bite. It was a relatively new growth, as far as she could tell, except for one distinct, crooked bend at the middle of the shoot—like her own index finger. Boldly, now, she looked back to the trunk in search of an answer to the riddle.

It was then that she saw it: a knar or—was it possible?—a dark brown eye, there in the opening of the bark, deep and dreamy, looking back at her.

It was 3:15. In just fifteen minutes, she was due to pick up Adam in Madison Park, and she was way up in the middle of Central Park's north end. She dashed east across the Meadow and was breathless by the time she tripped onto the sidewalk of 5th Avenue. But there was no way, even with the most reckless cab driver, that she could make it down to 25th street in time. Her heart pounded with the terror that her son would feel as, one by one, all the children left, each with a parent or a babysitter, while only he remained. It was nearly 4:00 when she bounded out of the taxi and saw Adam's face, white as a sheet. It was what they'd always feared, come true at last, that he would find himself without her. In a sweat, she flung open the playground gate, its clatter catching the attention of the little group around her son, their faces smiling with relief.

"Mama! Did you forget me?" asked Adam, seeing in her eyes that something had happened to her that afternoon. He forgave her on the spot, sensing the importance of the day and how it had made his Mama seem older, yet also younger, but all that mattered was that she was holding his hand. He saw her thank the Scientist and Charlie and her mother Paulette, who had all stayed with Adam until Emma got there. They all went their separate ways as Adam gripped his mother's hand tighter, exhausted from the anguish of her absence. Coming out of dreams and terrors, she found herself being led to the very real place of the Shake Shack, and before she could protest, found herself next in line at the outside counter. They found an empty table and attacked their big chocolate ice cream cones. They were licking the sticky drips from their fingers when Adam asked her about the muddy drips on her legs (she must have been a sight, breaking from the woods like a scared animal), and she responded with a smile and nodded but said nothing. Instead, she told him all about her boat trip across the Lake, and the Hooded Warbler that darted in and out of the Hackberry tree (he laughed at the word, just like she knew he would), and the silver bat that flew right past her in broad daylight, and her walk through the Meadow, and the quiet of the woods. Adam listened with wonder and relief that he didn't have to go on that long hike. Soon they both were silent with their thoughts. Adam crawled into his mother's lap, and she wrapped her arms around him. The canopy of branches above them barely moved in the still air but cast substantial shadows that protected them from the late August sun. There they stayed until the early evening, huddling in that shady spot.

It was time for bed. Adam brought his mother one of his mythology books, and the gods and centaurs, nymphs and satyrs appeared before them, released in flight across a canvas, or strangely fleshlike in marble stance, breathing fear, great deeds, or amorous intent. Emma watched over his shoulder as he flipped through the pages, stopping to comment on a picture of Argos, the sentry with a hundred eyes. "They could have painted it from *his* point of view," Adam said with compassion for Hera's slave, who always had to sleep with some eyes open to guard Io, the beautiful princess. Poor Io! She was never safe, Adam sighed, sensing the drama in the Bloemaert rendition, and remembering pieces of the story, was eager to talk about it with his mother.

"Sometimes love is a mighty thing," Emma began. "After all, Io and Zeus loved each other. Zeus was just trying to protect the priestess from Hera's anger. Remember? That's why Zeus disguised himself as a huge cloud that darkened the world. When Hera broke through that puffy disguise and found them, Zeus quickly changed Io into a cow. Hera was crafty and demanded that Zeus give her the cow as a gift, pretending she didn't know it was Io. Zeus had no choice but to watch Hera chain his beloved to an olive tree, where she could only wander several feet. Then Hera placed the hundred-eyed watchman there, who was ever ready to tackle Zeus should he come sweeping down to set her free."

But Adam did remember, all too vividly. "It was bad enough," he went on, "that Io was turned into a cow, but look what happened to poor Argos! Zeus waited until he could hardly stay awake. Then he sent Hermes to tell him *he* would watch the cow so Argos could sleep. Then, with all hundred eyes asleep, Hermes kills him!"

"Yes, it's not fair that some people, or gods, decide the fate of others. But maybe the myth is not really about that, but about the power of feelings."

"They shouldn't be *that* powerful, to change a girl into a cow! Anyway, if I made that painting, I would make Argos's eyes different. Here some are open and some are closed, but they don't tell you anything."

"What do you think they should say?"

"His eyes should show how tired he is and how afraid he is to close them. Here he's just a giant with a hundred eyes."

"The painting needs to show how much it matters to stay awake or fall asleep. Is that what you're saying?"

"Yes, everything matters, the cow, the cloud, all the eyes."

It was getting late, but just as Emma was about to take the book from Adam's hands, he became enthralled by the Bernini sculpture of Apollo and Daphne—Emma's favorite.

Adam was peering at the bottom, studying Daphne's toes, which seemed to be turning into roots clutching the ground. Emma started telling him the story, but he got stuck on the part about Eros's arrows and how he shot them through the air at Daphne and Apollo, and how exactly did that work?

"Eros was the god of love and could give people strong feelings for each other. One day, Apollo—who was a great warrior—made fun of Eros and his bow and arrows, saying that he had no business with weapons, only love. Eros was so angry he decided to get revenge. He dipped the tip of one of his arrows in gold and shot Apollo with it. It made Apollo love the first creature he laid eyes on. As the story goes, it was Daphne. Then Eros took a second arrow and dipped its tip into lead. He shot Daphne with it, and it made her want to flee the first person she saw, and that was Apollo."

"So gold is love, and lead is hate?"

"Well, Daphne doesn't hate Apollo, but she's *repelled* by him. It's like your magnets. Some of them contain the force of attraction. They can't help but stick to each other. Others do just the opposite. They push each other away. Now, Daphne was different from many nymphs in that she was *already* repelled. She didn't want anything to do with *any* man, no matter *who* it was, even a god. She wanted to stay forever in the woods, to hunt with the goddess Artemis."

"Like a child. She didn't want to grow up. But what happened, Mama?" Adam asked, staring at the statue. "Apollo has his hand around Daphne, but her hair is flying away from him and her mouth is open, just like in my dream."

"What dream?"

"The one I had when I tried to scream and there was no sound."

"Yes! She's horrified that Apollo is about to grab her, but she doesn't realize that at that very minute, her father, Peneus, hears her silent scream."

"How can he hear something silent?"

"Well, he heard her thoughts. Daphne was wishing so hard for protection. Just as Apollo was about to grab her, her father turned her into a laurel tree. He's a river god and has powers of his own."

Adam studied the sculpture intently.

"It looks like her fingers are turning into branches, and bark is growing around her body."

Emma thought that this must scare him.

"No, Mama, I'm okay," he said, reading her mind.

"But you were so scared when Professor Lupin turned into a werewolf! How is one kind of metamorphosis different from another? Is it because the werewolf is such a scary animal?"

"No, it's because Daphne's father was only trying to protect her. He wasn't mean or anything like that. But it isn't fair."

"What isn't, Adam?"

"He should have changed *Apollo* into a tree, not Daphne! It wasn't *her* fault."

"No, it *isn't* fair. But the thing is, Apollo is a god, and metamorphosis doesn't work on a god."

"But you said Zeus turned into a cloud!" He was becoming agitated.

"That's right, but he turned *himself* into the cloud, and only for a moment. Poor Io, who was a girl, was turned into a cow forever."

"I guess Daphne will never change back, will she, Mama?"

Exhausted from the day's emotions, Adam lay back on the pillow, imagining the river god, his head bent in sadness near his child tree, gone from him forever. Emma turned off the light and, from across the room, looked toward her son, lost in the darkness of the unlit room. He turned and looked back at her, his dark eyes luminous in the shadow. It was then that it came to her: The eye that had opened from her brow that morning in the midst of sleep was none other than her child's, its gaze deep and dark, that would behold the world when she was gone.

PART THREE

I. Alice

In the spring and summer months, it was not so easy to see clear across to the other side of Washington Square. The old elms, maples, and chestnuts were full with age, their small green hands cupping all the air, leaving little room for the sun, let alone a piece of sky. But now it was late autumn, that time of year when one could see their naked limbs, crooked and strong, tapering off into slender twigs where some leaves still clung, clutching at the mast as the wind picked up, and fluttering red and orange in the low sunlight. Alice could wander about in the solitude of trees, fragrant with leaves scattered below, smoky and crunchy, dancing over hidden roots like children on a grave. There was nothing more beautiful to her than to look west across the Square at sunset into the deepening blues and pinks, caught in the grip of ink-black branches that seemed to hold up the sky. She found herself entirely clasped by limbs and clouds; the rumbling of cars and other urban sounds were stilled.

She made her way slowly up Washington Square East. The last shrieks of laughter from the playground floated playfully away into the dimming sky as children pumped with all their might on their last swing rides of the day. It had grown cold at that hour, though it wasn't the air that chilled them, but the cries of littler ones being whisked away against their will from the sandbox and forced into their strollers. The big iron gate swung open: playtime was over. Parents and nannies beckoned to the last kids airborne. There was nothing as good as flight, to let go of the ground and leap out with a rush into space, higher than the trees, higher than a kite! But even the birds that migrate by night, hidden from the deftest trackers, must come down to rest. The rusty chains accompanied the children to the end with a deep squeak here, as their feet touched the sky, and a deep squeak there, as they swung back the other way. And so, with a reluctant toe dragging the ground until the swing came to a wobbly halt, each child came back down to earth. Alice loved the ones who put up the biggest fight, leaving the Square with the secret of their strength.

It was on such an autumn night that Alice's mother had yelled to her to come down from the tire swing where she was flying on defiantly, long after the stars had come out. She was eleven by then, and it would still be a few years before she ceased to return, day after day, to the easy sway above the grass and the embrace of trees. It was the first night that her father hadn't come home. There was no phone call, no word from him at all. His secretary said he left the office at 4:30 for an appointment. Jenna was unable to rise from the kitchen table, where she looked out the window at the empty driveway as the minutes turned into hours.

Time was becoming increasingly elusive. The Dr. Seuss branches—feathery, whimsical—waved at her from the yard. How to wave back? She was uneasy. Those same trees, and the wind blowing through them, were almost strangers. There had been a steady glow thrown on the world, warming her for years, with the simple presence of this girl, Alice, and that man, Hank. It was all she ever wanted, to love with ease and laugh with ease. To just be. Birthdays came and went with Jenna waltzing in with cake after cake, her smile wider than the proud chocolate tiers on the ceramic plate. This was no cliché, Jenna thought. It was her very song, uninterrupted.

How raw the air now in these shadows, this greyness all over the yard. Hank's absence made her feel homeless. This house couldn't last... Her daughter's stubborn defiance came into view as she swayed on the swing, as if a silent plea to the wind. Jenna watched Alice move energetically forward, then back again, sadly receding. She didn't know how to comfort her. She was even a little afraid of Alice's fierce emotion. Jenna felt helpless, inconsequential.

Did they even know her, husband or daughter? God knows she loved them! But how swiftly connective feeling at once inhabits the soul! So familiar... that rawness in the air. Atmospheric particles hummed around her now, just as when she played the violin. At her most raw, she would exist in the grip of a piece that lifted her out of her very skin. Ravished by sound, she felt an opening and a deepening of all those wells she couldn't name. Only sound, only music, could name her heart, decode her emotion. She would journey out of all confines and would return with the minor bruises of ecstasy.

She stopped playing when she met Hank, overcome by shyness. Why the big secret, and was there even one? The simple ease of life seemed to be enough for her; she had always reached for it and would give up anything to have some of that. But in that grey hour, heavy with thought, she wondered if there were parts of herself that had always remained inaccessible to Hank, even if, on the face of it, he was gone from her, a little more each time, in his stupors and his fugues. She knew her self-protective instinct was a necessity. The idea emboldened her with the vague conviction that she must and would find her way. She didn't need to play the violin again. It was all too emotional. She only wanted to feel at ease. She hung on to that thought.

Alice had been in the yard since 3:00. Finally, the early November chill got the better of her. She burst into the house with fiery cheeks and pangs of hunger. Within the few seconds it took to ask after her father, she understood, in the deepest way, that there was no news, then returned in silence to the swing.

She embraced the logic of emotion up there, rocking to and fro in the sky. If she stayed aloft, it would not be true that Hank wasn't coming home, or, for that matter, that something was terribly wrong between him and Jenna. She referred to them by name when she was fed up with their common weakness. But Alice knew better. She had felt them falling away from each other for some time, bit by bit, going down without a fight—unlike herself, who would stay up there all night if she had to. Her mother came out to join her in the yard, but the girl kept on swinging, leaving Jenna's cries to sift through the trees. Well, somebody had to do something! Jenna, ashamed of her helplessness and unable to stand the cold any longer, muttered that she was going in to get warm, leaving her daughter alone but for the stars blinking at her through the branches.

Close to midnight, she heard the hush of careful footsteps amid the faint crackle of leaves and slowed down her pace as a figure emerged in the dark. Her heart quickened, then skipped a beat altogether. She knew it was her father, but his shape looked unfamiliar in the faint glow of the moon. His ridiculous fur hat attenuated the stealthy gait and the hungry look in his eye, unfamiliar to her. He was clearly heading for the back door, in an effort to maintain the quiet that shrouded the house and avoid a scene till morning. Mattie, who slept atop the back of the couch just beneath the bay window, keeping guard throughout the night, could not be fooled, hearing deep into the silence, and howled in warning. About to hurry in to quiet the dog, Hank was drawn back out by the creaking sound above and followed the sound into the backyard trees. Alice swung out of reach as Hank moved toward her, then unavoidably back the other way as he groped for the rope, twisted by her frightened flight. He was unsteady but determined to bring her down.

"Get down from there, Alice, NOW!" Hank barked. He'd been drinking and smoking for hours with Gloria, a friend from work, who made it a point never to talk about herself, which Hank respected. At times, her quick wit betrayed unspeakable sadness. Lost in thought about her, he didn't see the swing coming at him, and it crashed against his shoulder, and he stumbled to the ground.

"Why *should* I? *You're* home late, so why can't *I* stay out?" Alice shouted back as Hank struggled to his feet, exasperated by his lack of authority, not that he really wanted any. He glared back at her. As she met his gaze defiantly, he was overcome by just how close he felt to her despite the war between them. His face softened, and Alice felt drawn to him, remorseful, and longing quickened her breath, and her agitation got the better of her travels. She peered into the treetops, not knowing whether to stay up there in the protective fold of branch and trunk or come down to her father's outstretched arms. The pendulum slowed just enough for Hank to catch hold of the rope. He grabbed her from behind and gripped her in a wobbly hug as the swing jerked to a stop. Alice slid out of his grasp and, as she touched ground, felt the earth sink slightly, then lost her balance. Hank caught her by the arm; her eyes met his a second time, imploring him to not let go.

Someone in the playground called her name and broke the hush of memory. It was Adam, the last one on the swings—his grin wider than the Cheshire Cat's—who, finally getting her attention (he'd called to her at least twenty times!), jumped down, ran through the gate, and piled into her arms, pressing an icy cheek against her face. Emma, looking grateful, followed close behind.

"Thank goodness you arrived! He would never have come down from that swing. He can stay up there for hours!"

Feeling content with himself and the way he mastered his mother, he rested his head on Alice's shoulder, refusing to come down from this warmer height, suddenly tired from all the swinging and the falling night.

They were walking along in silence when a rustling in the shadows made Alice jump, and quickly set Adam down, then turn back toward the sound with a concerned face.

"What's the matter?" Adam whispered whitely. Emma saw him tremble and she picked him up, her own heart racing, while Alice stood there, frozen in her tracks.

"Is it the werewolf?" he whispered still more fearfully. The rustling grew louder then stopped completely as a pair of tree squirrels dashed out of the bushes, leapt onto the nearest trunk and scampered up into the black treetops. Adam, Emma, and Alice burst into laughter.

"That was a close call, wasn't it, Mama?" Adam asked shakily, peering up into her eyes.

"Oh, Adam! There are no werewolves in the park!" she said, leaving him to ponder their real hiding-place—the woods, no doubt. He wanted to stay in her arms, even though her hurried pace disconcerted him. She was trying to quiet her own foreboding. Something was lurking, always was. The three friends left the Square and parted ways, Alice and Adam blowing each other kisses that puffed visibly in the cold air, disappearing as the distance grew between them.

Alice resumed her walk, more sadly now, turning west towards Waverly Place, along the Square's northern perimeter. The Arch sat clean and still behind the wire fence, glowing stoically before the ruins of construction. The heart of the park was inaccessible. The fountain had been dismantled; saplings were left under wraps beside great gouges in the earth, the dirt piled high and frozen. Hard to believe that thirty trees were axed—mature, centennial trees, destroyed because they were "in the way". More important to align the new fountain with the Arch! Alice was sick over it. Instinctively, she wandered back into the Square and stepped onto a beckoning trail, the only one she knew of below 14th Street—a trail formed on the closing of the Square's whole west side during "reconstruction", except for the chess tables at the southwest corner, and the baby park just west of the Arch. Urban wanderers unwilling to give up their zigzag jaunt across the Square had slowly but surely blazed this thirty-second trail from the north border to the center of the park, just outside the wrought-iron fence of the older kids' playground. Such stealthy stomping was not revenge enough for the meshy barricades that now blocked off the Square's west side, but it was gratifying anyway to feel the earth beneath your feet and, with any luck, it would be muddy.

All was quiet but for Alice, oddly solitary in the Square. She turned and followed the trail back out to the sidewalk and continued on her stroll. Within, the central fountain, now dismantled, offered no life source. Were it not for the trees! she whispered to herself. They bent over the sidewalk, heavy with impending winter, but she could smell the sap just the same and thought she could hear the waters coursing through their veins from the recent cold rain. She went on, quietly persevering like a monk in contemplation along the open galleries of the periphery, gazing at the planeted, starry sky—her vaulted ceiling. The ritual gave meaning to the night. Bereft all that autumn, Alice hurried on to find what solace there lay in the stroll.

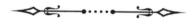

A vague awareness of something dark had started growing in her that season, born perhaps in the shadows of her apartment building, cast over the construction site of the World Trade Center. She would sit for hours at her window, gazing at the big yellow cranes that cranked their teeth in and out of the earth like dinosaurs foraging the blank terrain. At night, it would all come to a halt, and there the cranes would sit, suddenly inert, without a firefly in sight. It was, after all, some seven years since the Towers fell in, and the emptiness was just as loud as ever, forbidding anything at all to sprout. Just steps away, underground, the Cortland Street subway station remained inoperable, with subway cars screeching slowly past dusty walls branded with black Xs, weirdly luminous beyond a barricade of tape and tools left lying there. "Don't get off at Ghost Town," a voice whispered low. "If you do, you'll hear the cries," Alice replied to her own haunting.

Eventually, that wasteland scene became unbearable at night, and Alice would flee to the park along the Hudson, even when the winds were biting. The need to look out at some other vast expanse would urge her to the river, where she would hang over the iron railing and peer into the black waters, so devoid of light that there was no reflection of the sky, even moonlit, even starry. She must have looked into that inky void once too often; she began to notice that a thing as hard as a concrete sidewalk left almost no sensation under her feet—couldn't feel it, or rather, what she did feel was the lack of ground beneath her. It was an odd sensation, coming upon her emotionally when she came back to the city without Rodger in her life, and which was now intensified by this peering into the river; probing those currents for any hint at all about who she was and where she was going became futile in the wet nothingness. The last sensation of hard ground was soon undone. So bizarre was the sensation that Alice would have confined herself to her room had she not plucked up the courage to fight back, convinced at last that the more she walked around, the better the chance of recovering that sense of being on the ground. So she roamed the city here, then there, with the night's chill under her collar despite the heat—cranked as if it were Alaska—that filled the café where she would stop most nights on her journey back home.

She could forget all this with Adam, whom she watched in the late afternoon, once or twice a week, now that he was back in school. His spirit was contagious. Emma had confided to Alice that her child would fly into command the second he heard the doorbell ring, and exile his mother from the entrance. He would fling the door wide open and reach his arms up at the sight of Alice, who, in one fluid motion, would pick him up, throw down her jacket and kick off her shoes. He would point to his room, and away they went. He watched eagerly as Alice reached into her bottomless bag and pulled out a cluster of perfect torsos, slender limbs, and tresses of all colors. Adam had never seen such a collection of Barbies, looking on with wonder as a batgirl, or a princess, or a witch would appear out of the chaos of mingled bodies in Alice's hands. He would then throw off the top of his treasure basket and spill out his own collection of action figures, and his varied and heroic animals, always ready to whisk a hero in distress off to the clouds on the top bunk, where they would miraculously recover. Spilling from the cascade were the odd pieces of ribbon, acorns, and pebbles that had somehow got caught in the mix.

One day, when evening came on earlier than usual, Adam put down his flying dog with the cape and, looking up out the window, remarked that the world was sad. He then turned back to his toys with renewed vigor and proceeded to tie the Barbies and superheroes to the slats in the bed or attach them to any available lamp stem or chair leg, demanding that Alice give him more pieces of ribbon or string as he went along.

"Why are you tying them all up, Adam? Is somebody taking them prisoner?"

"I'm not tying them up!" he exclaimed as he fastened a super-girl to the headboard.

"Well, then, what *are* you doing?" asked Alice as Emma came into the room.

"Can't you see? They're afraid that there's no more gravity. They can't keep themselves on the ground."

He turned an inquisitive face toward his mother.

"And you did well to watch over them, Adam," Emma responded. She led Alice gently out of the room, wondering to herself about the meaning of his curious game and the anxious look on Alice's face. Emma had been sensing something adrift, or distracted, in Alice as the autumn headed into winter. There was something so still and opaque in the final days of the season. From time to time, they talked about Alice's last year in the art program and what lay beyond. The girl had no idea. She looked back toward Adam's room as he called out to reassure her that the creatures were all safe now and wouldn't drift off into space. Alice decided to leave her dolls there with him in the hope of finding them on solid ground next week.

As she gathered her things to go and approaching Emma to schedule her next visit, Alice noticed her teacher's fingers black with soft pencil dust. She'd been hard at work on a series of drawings since the end of September, she confided in Alice, who shyly asked if she could see them. Emma led her to the studio and pointed to three drawings on the table, told her she could stay as long as she wanted, then went off to look in on Adam.

Alice had never been inside Emma's studio, but from the doorway had glimpsed her teacher focusing intently on the paper before her, fruits and vegetables, and the stalks of plants scattered about. The whole room seemed to hum with the tension of this human encounter with remnants of nature, which continued to linger, as if it existed, on its own; the air was abuzz. Alice sensed almost a dreamlike quality about the room. She could never have felt that in a gallery, remembering the drawings in a recent one-woman show of Emma's. There was, nevertheless, something that lifted off the paper; the still lifes seemed to be reaching for something. She found herself thinking about those drawings long after—

the strength of the carrot, the decomposition of the rancid peach. But most of all, it was the pepper that gripped Alice with its uneasy beauty. She remembered it as green despite the absence of color, its lively bumps and folds, rendered with the subtlest gradations of light, were juxtaposed with parts unfinished, a thin quiet line evoking the rest of that pepper with such delicacy that the eye, in response, compensated, completing the pepper in spaces without line, then, with a blink, falling off into the void: the thing found, then lost again, that simply cannot keep still—that lingers, vivid, like a dream, but then is gone again, so quickly.

Before Alice there now lay three drawings, larger than the other works she'd seen. It turned out they were studies for work on a still larger scale. Some pale cream and other faintly earth-colored papers, which Emma made herself, lay drying in the back between a giant mesh mold and a deckle. There was a woodsy smell in the room, emanating from the damp sheets. Alice returned to the drawings lying on the long table, set distinctly apart from each other. Dated October 10th, November 15th, with the third undated, they appeared to be a series. Alice quickly scanned the room; there were no vegetables in sight.

Peering over the first drawing, all Alice could make out at first were shades of darkness and a curious glow. She felt herself adjusting her vision to the spectrum of the drawing as if she were awakening in a room at night and slowly making out the objects around her. What she saw eventually were roots, some thick and full, others tapered, elbowing their way through the earth but also jutting out above ground on what looked like a trail. While Alice could distinguish between the surface and the underground world, they were not exposed as such, nor was it clear if it was night or day. A light source from small unshaded areas lingering at the uncertain break between above and below ground revealed roots glowing faintly here and there, above and below. The light source did not make sense as she knew it, but illuminated in ways that cut unpredictably through space and time. Alice found herself searching for the tree trunk, but to no avail: this was a drawing of roots, in all their forcefulness.

It seemed to have rained not too long ago. Above ground, the trail was cramped with the violence of growth that would've made for an uneasy hike; below, the earth looked bottomless, taking Alice back to the Hudson's edge, and the nightly waters that drew her in. Liquid darkness is the most vertiginous of all, even more than black air, in the dead of night, when one wakes up to nothingness, but that saves you from free fall, holding out the promise of the edge of a mattress, a hard floor, a door to open. But at the Hudson there was no such promise. She did not want to linger there and kept looking for ways to fight off the urge to stay. She finally tore herself away from those roots which seemed to break through the flat dimension of the paper and into the room, or at least a little too thoroughly into her dream space.

The second drawing was just as disorienting, especially in terms of perspective. It took Alice a moment to realize that she was looking at the base of an uprooted tree whose sprawling trunk rested horizontally on a similar forest trail and which lay for the most part unseen, hidden by the complex hub of roots that had jerked themselves out of the ground and into the air. The spatial confusion lay in the use of soft and hard pencils that captured light in jarring ways. The roots exposed to the sun looked somehow deep and dark, even in their contact with the air, while those closer to the trunk continued to sinew like snakes coiling in the light, inverting the behavior of shadows. The effect was more brutal, as in this uprooting, and unnatural, as in a tree turned up on itself.

"Really in your face," she breathed aloud, and tried to imagine what force could have thrown down such a heavy trunk. Can the wind do that? You forget, living in the city. But hundreds of trees had been knocked down all over Central Park some months before by a ravaging storm with gusts up to 80 miles an hour. Limbs were snapped off, giant American elms over 100 feet high were split through the trunk and cracked off onto the green, and, yes, many trees uprooted. Hard to believe there's a force stronger than trees. But as she gazed at Emma's drawing, Alice realized that the roots seemed to curl around themselves, like countless legs crossed Indian-style. These roots actually gathered themselves into a relatively flat system. Was it a myth, then, that roots burrowed deeper and deeper into the ground over time, going even lower than the tree was high? That's what she'd always thought and didn't want it to be otherwise. But as she looked at Emma's drawing, she found a truth equally compelling, and that compensated for her lost illusion: *all roots were not the same.* They worked in a system; those outside of the ring were small and wet, like tiny drinking straws sucking up minerals and water, while those closer to the trunk were thick and heavy, anchoring the tree at its base. The roots seemed to breathe, which is why they didn't dive so very deep into the earth, but elbowed out near the base. Later that night, Alice went to the library to verify this; it was, after all, a drawing and not necessarily realistic. She found that Emma's drawings were imbued with an exact botany of this underground system. But they exceeded the botanical in their reach for the inner life of roots.

She turned to the third drawing, clearly unfinished, but the pencil was hardly timid. Here was a stump, still sappy, of a young pine, thrown upwards as if from the blow of an ax. Alice thought of Audubon's birds, the artist trying to capture them in life, painting frenetically after he shot them. Not that Emma had cut down that tree. But someone had, for this was not the doing of the wind. How long does a tree ooze sap after it's axed, she wondered. Days? Years? Here it looked thick and frosty as if a sudden chill had blown through, freezing some drips midway. But it's only autumn, Alice noted from the color of the leaves—realizing then that she was seeing color in a black and white drawing, unconsciously perceiving bright hues of violence in the scene. Why the chill? The dawn light was dim; it roused with no warmth, leaving things to fend for themselves. She hears the ax fall, a dog bark, then birds flutter up like a grey cloud sucked back into the sky; branches crackle followed by an eerie silence, and she comes upon the stump...

The triangle of branches and needles tapered off to the side on the forest floor, but it was the stump that the drawing arrested in dumb shock. This was different from anything she had ever seen in Emma's drawings. Here was the work of sheer human brutality. Alice looked around the studio for other signs. A sketch of an index finger, vulnerable, floated in the space of some paper tacked to the wall. She grew queasy and turned back to the stump, jutting up from the forest floor, transfixed in the air: *a stump in the void.* There was no floating or dangling here, just pure severance, in confrontation with nothing.

It had been a perpetual autumn, and Alice was caught, now more than ever, in midair.

Adam looked up quickly from the game he'd been playing, surprised by a sudden creak and bang: the apartment door had swung open and closed. "When is Alice was coming back?" he called to his mother, only half-expecting a reply.

It was only a week after Thanksgiving, but Christmas had already settled on the city. Not that Alice minded much; there were few things she liked more than colored lights. She used to go driving with Pam every year at Christmastime and look at the decorations in the neighborhood. She secretly loved them all, from the few twinkling lights in a sticker bush to the total casino effect, as if she'd just pulled into downtown Vegas. The girls would laugh at the gaudy mangers glowing in the dark and the electric Santas burning on quiet lawns like red and white torches. It always amazed Alice that the houses seemed deserted. Where was everybody? What was the point of all those decorations if nobody came out to look at the brightly lit lawns up and down the block; or at least stand out there and take in the glowing colors on, in, and around one's house? That was one great thing about Hank. He would sit out on the porch for hours in his wool hat, plaid jacket, and weathered mittens, sipping tea from his favorite mug. Alice would keep him company until her ears froze.

"What are you two doing out there?" Jenna would yell from the bedroom window.

"Looking at Christmas!" they'd call back in unison. Alice would imagine her mother shrugging and then stealing into bed, closing her eyes with a faint smile on her lips.

With cheery anticipation, Alice headed to the Washington Square Arch to see the Christmas tree, which they had raised and lit up a few days earlier. Her gaze slid slowly down the tree, taking in the bright white star at the top, then at the de-lightful fiery eggs glowing red and green and amber in the piney skirts. It came to her that they were some kind of imitation pinecones, as if the tree were coming back, electrically alive, a cyborg of sorts. Her eyes then rested at the base, which reached out of the tiles in an illusion of roots below, the barren trunk thrust hidden but inches into the earth.

The whole block smelled of sap, plunging Alice back into the Pinelands, where she used to go every autumn as a child and run like a savage till she fell over with exhaustion. She could still feel between her teeth that grainy texture of "sugar sand" that her father lovingly called the white-ish forest floor, to the acute disappointment of the child who spit it out in shock upon discovering—once it got into her mouth— that it was only sand, mixed with dirt, with no candy to be had. But the memory that gripped her now had to do with a particular adventure when she was nine, alone in the woods with her mother, and a cacophony of bird calls. Alice spotted a sweet little pine warbler on the branch of a grand pitch, and quickly calculated how easy it would be to shimmy up the trunk and boost herself up onto one of the branches jutting out some five feet from the ground. By this time, the warbler had made its way to some spot out of sight, leaving in its wake a trail of trills. Alice thought she would replace the bird on a high branch, imagining herself calling trium- phantly to her mother below. But the climb was harder than she thought, and halfway up, she stopped to catch her breath, nestling her cheek against the scented bark. Nothing smelled so good! Jenna, having finally reached the tree, peered up to find a creature perched in the branches, half- hidden by masses of needles and cones. Alice caught her mother's bewildered gaze and quickly scurried down, expect- ing to be greeted by the usual sigh of relief. But Jenna just stood staring at her.

"Mommy," Alice asked, "what's the matter?"

Without a word, Jenna held up Alice's long braids with the tips of her fingers. "Your hair is full of sap!" They would have gotten over it when they got home if Jenna's fine comb hadn't broken its teeth on the crusty clumps. She grabbed scissors to tame the wild head once and for all.

"Mommy, don't," begged Alice, pulling back and falling to the floor. But she quickly picked herself up and, standing as tall as she could, looked Jenna squarely in the eyes. The braids were spared. Alice promised to shampoo twice a day until all the sap was out. Pausing now under the Arch, she slowly pulled her fingers through her hair as if there might still be some trace.

Looking up, she saw a bold escapee from the Christmas tree, hovering between the moon and the Arch. But it was only the Red Planet shining in the night sky of the city. Alice felt oddly serene there in the silent Square, despite the wire fence that loomed forbiddingly nearby. She walked over to look at the construction site more closely and discovered a huge, gaping hole. Since her last visit, the entire fountain in the middle of the Square had been dismantled. It had been plowed down to a mere stump of a thing, with overturned marbled ruins sticking out every which way in what was now an outdoor storage space. Those fountain fragments shone a dull grayish-yellow in the pall of a portable light tower. Disgusted, Alice, in a last act of resistance, resumed her stroll around the Square's perimeter. Behind her, the Christmas tree twinkled on, impervious.

At the northwest corner, she came upon a regal figure: the great English elm, standing tall and solemn. Over three centuries old, it had outlived all the elms in Manhattan, including two of its brothers in the Square itself. There were few things in her life more constant. Without its dark green leaves—lush from April through October—it looked wicked, with its craggy bends and hair-like twigs splintering out into the sky. Looking at the elm's gigantic lower branch—which jutted out, straight and sure, then curved abruptly downward, pointing at the earth—Alice thought of Rodger on a stroll with her around the Square, when they stopped in fascination at the tree—what did he call it? *Hangman's elm.* The deathly association of the branch was unmistakable, now naked of leaves, steadfast behind the authority of the metal fence. Alice cringed at the thought of traitors flailing, neck in noose, during the days of the Revolution.

She felt it in her feet and heard it in the wind. As she looked up at the leafless elm, that scene returned. It was now that night again when Hank came home so late, his gaze altered somehow—she could see it when he reached for her as she dangled on the tire swing, the rope creaking as she swung away in terror, then plunged back through the air toward this man who was her father. She fell backwards and off the swing, her back bending starkly in an arch and wavering near his arms that opened to catch her. When she hit the ground, the earth sunk ever so slightly beneath her feet, and all went dark, for seconds, or years, as in a dreamless sleep.

She threw her backpack over the wire fence, scrambled over it and down into the forbidden Park. The elm stood before her with its huge base and double trunk that shot into the sky. Two gigantic limbs had berthed hundreds of smaller branches reaching out across the path toward the east, and, westward, overflowing onto the Square's perimeter. Alice gasped at the sight of it, then, suddenly exhausted, slumped down next to it, leaning all her weight against the trunk, relieved to feel something solid, bigger than herself. She huddled closer still—it was so cold out there—then noticed an odd, earthy smell, faintly sweet, like the vapors from the first crush of grapes. It was as if something were fermenting in the trunk; and then, looking closely, she saw that there was something slightly oozing from a long triangular gash, rising just above the base. The old elm was a major figure in her personal landscape; it couldn't possibly be rotting or diseased. This was surely some kind of wound, and Alice imagined that it could be dressed and healed.

Shivering, she looked up at the treetops shimmering in the wind, her gaze soon returning to the elm and falling upon what looked like a very large ear, hollowed into the blackened bark of the trunk some 15 feet up on its northern side. It appeared, it seemed, from an unconscious longing for such a preternatural presence, attuned to the troubled sounds, inarticulate, yet understood. Considering her possibilities, she climbed onto an overturned picnic table and, with a determined leap, caught hold of a thick branch and pulled herself up into the limbs. She climbed further up, sure-footed, until she reached the southern trunk and stood up gingerly, trying to avoid the twigs that managed to catch themselves in her face and hair. It was a good three feet to Hangman's branch and a precipitous drop below. Pressing herself into the bark and the vast trunk as best she could, she edged out onto the branch with her right foot, then quickly pulled her left next to it. She ran her hands along the scaly bark, the deep old grooves giving it a cork-like feel.

She loved everything about the tree, its texture and its mighty height and fanning crown. Sweaty and satisfied, she crouched against the trunk, curling forward with her limbs pulled into her chest, circular and serene within the crook of the trunk and the branch, just at the height of the big gnarly ear. She sat exhaling chilly grey clouds into the black air. She felt altogether planted there, an outgrowth of the tree, and took in the stillness, that is until a frightened squirrel broke the air with its scream. Alice squirmed still closer to the trunk and pressed her face against her thighs, fearing some searchlight might pause upon her blinking eyes and expose her crime. There was in fact a cop roaming the southern edge of the Square, making his rounds. Her heart was pounding, yet she felt content—never so content as at that moment. The cop, now out of sight, she rested her cheek against the bark and cocked her head toward the ear. A passerby would take her whispers for the wind.

But her father would know. And this time, if he were to beckon from below, she would choose the tree.

II. Adam

"How many more years of school do I have left?" yelled Adam, struggling with a sock that couldn't care less if he had five toes instead of four, which was all he could fit into it. He was precariously squatting on one foot, the other raised, and teetered with the effort, then fell over on his back. Usually this would have amused him, but getting these socks on was now no laughing matter, as he imagined Daddy scolding him for being late *again*. Maybe if his foot dove down into the sock, he would have more luck. So he stood up on his left leg and held the sock below his other, but just as he was about to slip in all his toes he lost his balance and fell face forward on the pillow that he'd tossed on the floor in an attempt to make his bed, and which was luckily waiting for him. But the sock was not the problem. The problem was school. No matter how many times he walked in and ran out of that kindergarten classroom, it didn't get any easier. Or, maybe it was a little easier, he had to admit, with some days better than others, and his friends were so funny that it was probably worth it.

"Hold on a second!" Luke called back distractedly from behind the *Times*, transfixed by a story about two Acadian peregrine falcons sighted on the ledge of the Chrysler Building. How did those diving raptors, whose nests were scraped into the flanks of Acadia's highest peaks, end up in the concrete city?

"We'll have to go and take a look," Luke said aloud.

"Look at what? How many are there?" Adam repeated, trying to calculate the exact number of years he had to go.

"I think there's only two," replied his father, in reference to the falcons.

"Oh, good; two is all I could stand."

"You can't stand *falcons*?" Luke retorted. Adam sat blinking at his bedroom floor. Falcons? What did his father mean?

Luke glanced up from the newspaper towards Adam's room just as a blue sock flew out the door and wished his son would just get ready for school without all the fuss. He looked forward to the moment when Emma and Adam would run out the door so he could be alone with his manuscript. He felt uneasy wishing they would go, but a deadline was a deadline. Where *was* Emma, anyway?

She was on the rocky shore behind the house at the Cove; the splash of the shower against the ceramic tub recalled the gentle murmur of low tide on that quiet beach. She was startled by a bald eagle swooping down from a nearby cliff, its talons pointed at the sea, where they momentarily disappeared in a shallow plunge, then resurfaced with a silvery blue mackerel in their grip. But other sounds now brought her back to family matters, with husband and son arguing more loudly than usual—about falcons of all things—just outside the bathroom door. She jerked off the faucet, eager to join in that conversation.

"Adam!" she called, drying off in a hurry, realizing with a glance at the clock that her daydreaming had gotten the better of her. "The bald eagle is practically the only enemy of the peregrine falcon," in an attempt to convince him that the falcon was a bird worthy of awe, not to be dismissed out of hand.

"What does that have to do with my sock or school?" Adam bellowed back.

Confused, though amused, by his retort, she didn't give it much credence, and this was usually her mistake, as she was all too often eager to teach him about things she cared about and not sensing if it were necessarily the right moment. While the thought made her squirm, her excitement got the better of her, once again. "What you won't learn in school is how amazing it is that peregrine falcons even exist on Mount Desert Island," she continued. "At one point, they all died out..."

"Right, right," Luke interrupted, wishing she'd stop talking and get going but equally intent on sharing the dramatic news of the Metro Section. For that moment, at least, Acadia was exactly in their backyard. "Acadian peregrines were spotted here, in New York City, on the Chrysler Building! Only Adam doesn't seem to like them."

"NOBODY LOVES BIRDS MORE THAN I DO!" the child shouted back as he slammed his bedroom door in frustration, then paused to wonder if he actually loved birds more than he loved snakes. He was thinking he would be a herpetologist when he grew up. The problem was that so many things intrigued him that he wished he could be ten different people at once so he wouldn't have to choose, or, more likely, could live several centuries and be something different every fifty years. In the meantime, Chloe—the corn snake in his classroom—was so sweet and beautiful! He wondered if his parents would let him watch her for a few weeks in the summer. He would just beg them, and they would have to say yes. And then he remembered that someone from the Audubon Society was coming to his class that morning and thought that a bird would also make a good companion.

"How do they know the peregrines are from Acadia?" Emma whispered to Luke who was trying to open Adam's door. "Did someone get a picture of their bands?"

"I don't know, Emma," he snapped. He had no idea what she was talking about, and he didn't want to get into it, as Adam's bedroom door was stuck and he had to get to work. "What are we going to do *now*?"

"But how is it they would nest on the Chrysler Building with those gargoyles?" Emma went on, caught between her concern for the birds and getting Adam to school on time.

"What, they're scared of gargoyles? There aren't any in the wild!" Luke said, still pushing on the bedroom door.

"But that's just the point! They're gargoyles of *eagles*!"

"So?"

On the other side of the door, Adam was deep in a game he made up about a female fighter pilot, Lady Manhands, and a pirate, Dick Deadeye—a name so horrible that nobody would ever mess with *him*. Dick was the greatest marksman of the sea, although it did unsettle Adam to imagine the globby wound behind the eye patch. His parents' conversation wafted through the wall and roused him from his game.

"Dad!" he yelled as Luke burst through the door.

"Here I am!" his father answered with relief.

"No! not you! The eagles!"

"The what?"

"The eagles! They prey on peregrine falcons!"

"So?"

"So that's why mom is surprised!"

Luke stared at him, and Adam waited to see if he'd catch on. As far as Adam was concerned, his father was the smartest person in the world. His mother was a different kind of smart, especially when it came to trees or understanding the things that he had trouble telling anybody else. She even knew before he told her—sometimes before he even knew himself—that he was thinking about something. But the truth was, and it was getting harder to hide it, that there really wasn't anybody he liked to talk to more than his father, especially about history and books and movies. It seemed like there wasn't anything his father *didn't* know. So why couldn't he answer a simple question about falcons?

"*Dad!* Would peregrine falcons perch on a building where there are eagles?"

"But they're not real.

"And are buildings *cliffs*?" Emma retorted.

Luke found it fascinating that those falcons ended up in New York City in the first place. He thought, maybe wrongly, that some differences were so essential that you couldn't reconcile them. Obviously, buildings were not cliffs. But the fact remained that those Acadian birds were there, on the ledge of the Chrysler Building. This conundrum was more boggling than the fact that the birds were nesting between the eagles' talons. Surely, Acadian Peregrine Falcons would know the difference between real eagles and gargoyles, between flesh and stone. These reflections brought him back to the eternal question of illusion and reality, which underscored the play that he was trying desperately to finish. The directors at Playtime were running out of patience. If there was any chance it would be staged next season, he would have to give them *Skyline* in its entirety. But he was stuck, tormented even, about how to end it. His main character, Walt, aspired to be a country singer, and dreamed of going to Tellico Plains, Tennessee, a place only as real to him as *Tellico*, a song he wrote, which sprang directly from the Bald River Falls that crashed out of a postcard a friend sent him, years ago. Walt never stopped looking at those Falls, and his reverie took him beyond, to the rolling plains and blue foothills of the Appalachian Mountains. Somehow, it all intermingled with an image of the Marlboro Man that was lodged deep in his psyche, calling him out West. "Tellico" was a breakthrough song, a big hit with the crowd at the Rock-wood, where he played Tuesday nights. The problem was how to get out of the New York City shelter system and move forward—and westward—with his life. Luke didn't want Walt to come off as crazy or simplistic, chasing after some impossible escape, but to convey the real condition of entrapment—the way class binds people to place. The myth of the great outdoors—of cowboy country—was an antidote to entrapment if, in the logic of that myth, you could only get out there and sit on that horse and look out at a boundless sky. Entrapment was real, and the West continued to retain a geographical openness that so many longed for, however illusory. At the turning point in the script, Walt reshapes the cityscape through a new genre all his own: country western

& rap ballads: *Uncrossed* (the East and Hudson Rivers), *Reservoir of Hope* (in Central Park), *Dredged-Up Dreams* (the Gowanus Canal), *Empire of Madness* (the Empire State Building) were the songs that came out of his wanderings through the city that still held him. Luke sought the pathos in his urban cowboy's plight, and yet did not want to romanticize him. His thoughts now drifted back to the falcons and the way they made do with a different skyline, with skyscraper cliffs, which was another case of disparate realities that merged.

Emma's concern lay with approximate realities. She remembered the cardinal in her backyard that used to fly from window to window as her mother went around the house. It was relentless, flying about like that, year after year, calling after her when she slipped out of sight. It would have been no problem if it hadn't kept on pecking at the window to get her mother's attention. One day, Emma's father, fed up, tacked a silhouette of a hawk onto the screen of their bedroom window. By the next morning, the bird had somehow *projectilely* crapped all over the fake predator. It was obviously enraged by the raptor cutout in its apparent symbolic dimension. What was it like, then, for those Peregrine Falcons perching near a fake but horrifying eagle's head? Perhaps they were making the ledge their territory and were trying to scare the bird away. Birds will mob their predators, like the herring gulls she saw on Baker's Island swooping down near an eagle and taunting it as it glanced about imperially from a boulder. Some birds could be fearless in the face of the enemy. But these falcons, nesting within the marble talons of the eagle, were another kind of fearless.

The Audubon clock that she had just put up in Adam's room startled everyone as it struck eight with the scratchy *o-ka-leeeee chit chit o-ka-leeee chit* of the Red-winged Blackbird. For Emma, the call was so evocative that the bird appeared before her with its shoulder patch of brilliant red, darting across the marsh like a tiny flame on a jet-black wing. Even that smallish bird would attack a raptor that came near its nest.

"Oh no!" Adam shouted. "We're going to be late!" In moments he was out the door, tripping down the hall with one sock half-on and no shoes. *School was actually going to be good that day*, he thought. "There's no way I'm gonna miss this!"

"Miss what?" Emma called out, running after him with coats and shoes. He had never been so eager to go to school.

"We're going to see birds of prey! Right up close! Some-one is coming to talk to us about raptors, and banding, whatever that is. *Let's go!*"

Adam hung on tightly to the hand that never failed to reach for his and hold it steadily no matter how long a walk they were on. Alice felt his grip tense up and pull back for a moment. The child was so excited about what lay above that he appeared to the girl poised to lift off, his arms extended behind him, wing-like. He was deep in thought. Would he actually see the fastest bird in the world scan the skies for prey, then swoop down at full speed? The Peregrine Falcon could go 200 miles an hour! It grabs its victim in mid-air, and then—Adam could hardly believe it—tosses it to its mate, the female, who swoops down beside him, only to turn upside down and catch it in her beak, in mid-air. Alice felt his grip relax again but sensed some sadness in his step, as he imagined the poor bird whose neck would break from the jolt of the Peregrine's wing. He tried to reason with himself that falcons needed to eat too, but he still felt bad anyway. But wait—Mama said that the Peregrine also had an enemy: the eagle. The idea that the falcon could be just as vulnerable as a starling gave him pause, but as they neared the Empire State Building, he cheered up again, excited to be going on this rocket-like adventure, way up to the Observation Deck on the 86th floor. There, he learned, one could see hundreds of birds as they began their springtime migration back up the east coast—some might even return to Acadia National Park. His own family was a lot like the birds, he thought, migrating to Maine every summer to the little house off Schooner Head Road and then back to the City for the winter.

Alice didn't hesitate to take him on this outing, although she'd never thought of visiting that landmark in all her years in New York City. On her nighttime rambles, the Empire State Building would glow like a lantern in cool green or royal purple against the black sky or shimmer white like a tall ghost in the fog. It was always something in the distance, unattainable, majestic, and a bit foreboding, its crown topped with an impossibly sharp needle as if about to pierce the invisible sac that held the heavens. Someday all the gods would come tumbling out, and how surprised she would be to have assumed she lived in a world of indifference.

It was a whole other thing actually to go inside that building and take the endless elevator to the top, where the colored lights illuminated the cubed tower top. It might be like entering a kaleidoscope—a symmetrical mystery best left unsolved, lest the brilliant colors turn out to be just so many bits of broken glass. And in the city's fabled "tallest building",—and most loved—that warm aura glowing at its peak might lose its mystery with the snapping flashes of tourists' cameras, blotting out the chance of seeing a shooting star, the awesome silence of the summit broken by meaningless chatter. But Alice never could refuse a climb up to the top of anything; and the thought of glimpsing all those fellow wanderers of the night flying through the air filled her with the kind of hope she hadn't known in months. Now, in mid-March, with spring just minutes away, she was all the more restless but also aimless, wishing she knew where to go. So *up* would have to do for now. She held Adam's hand still tighter as they wove through rush hour traffic and crossed to the other side of Fifth Avenue.

Adam scanned the sky one last time before passing beneath the canopy of steel. Dusk was falling, and some stray, deep white clouds were floating above. He had asked his dad to read the wind map just before he and Alice left the house. Luckily, it was blowing in from the northwest; otherwise they wouldn't see the birds. He had learned a lot from Andie, the naturalist who came to school a few days ago. She let him ask so many questions; he almost couldn't stop. He was sad that it wasn't October, when the birds migrated south over the city, the best time of all to go to the Observatory. But Andie had assured him that if the conditions were right, he just might see some raptors up there. After all, some of them had even made their homes in the city, much to Adam's surprise. *Wouldn't they like the cliffs and the ocean better than the tall buildings and streets?* Andie smiled kindly; she too found it mystifying. In their natural habitats they would also be safer from the blinding lights and glass that hurt the birds in mid-flight—the thought made Adam shudder. He'd stay far away from such a place!

"You'd think they would want to go back home after they flew south for the winter," he said aloud, knowing how much he would miss his room if *he* had to go away forever. But the need to eat seemed to be strongest of all for some of those birds; it was even stronger than their sense of home, and the city was one of the best places to hunt. The raptors were real city-dwellers, preferring to hang out on the streets and by the rivers. They scraped together homes in building overhangs or in frames of bridges, just like they did in nature.

They could swoop down to their hearts' content on smaller birds, mice or rats. And there were a lot of those fellows running around! Well, it seemed that some of these birds were immigrants. Adam marveled that they could feel so much at home in his world. What would his mother say when she learned that they wouldn't have to go to Maine that summer to see her animal friends? Many of them were right there in her own backyard, and she didn't even know it!

Leaving behind the hum of the city, they entered the skyscraper where everything, even *inside*, was tall: the ceilings, the map, the stairs, the guards. They made their way up to the second floor where the ascent began and wound their way around a path lined with burgundy velvet chains up to the security check, which they reached pretty quickly, since to Alice's great relief, there weren't many tourists there that evening. A few more long hallways and it was their turn! Adam's heart was racing as they rose a quarter of a mile into the sky. Everyone was silent. He wasn't sure why, but the elevator only went up to the 80th floor. They were so excited that they climbed up the last six flights rather than wait for the next car. Huffing and puffing, they made it to the top and stepped out into a world that seemed more imaginary than real, something like Dorothy and Toto stepping into the other side of the rainbow, or on top of it, he told Emma later that night.

Moving timidly onto the Observation Deck, Adam marveled first at the sky, which stretched out above like a great cloudy cloak, so pink that everything was glowing, especially the rooftops—obviously the most important thing about buildings, though you'd never know it if you never came up here. What? The Statue of Liberty couldn't possibly be so small! And what was that green patch over there? No! It couldn't be! Central Park? It took hours to cross it with Mama! From the Deck, the Park fit in his palm. With one small jump he would land on the other side. And what were those bug-like things below? When Alice told him they were cars he was so surprised he couldn't speak, which didn't happen often.

He wondered if things meant something else when they were much smaller. And when you looked up at a thing it was totally different than when you looked down at it. How did things become tall or small? And obviously, it made a difference how far away you were. Did things matter more if you were up close? Maybe that's why things on TV seemed so real, because he was looking close up at the screen. Was *The Prisoner of Azkaban* scary because he was up close? He'd ask Daddy about it. This might be what it meant to be a god—being able to see the world from as high up as Mount Olympus and come down sometimes when you fell in love with a human. Maybe that was why royalty sat on thrones, to be higher than everyone else, pretending to be gods. And what about the birds? From up high, the raptors probably thought they were the kings of the planet! He turned to Alice to remind her that they had to look out over the Hudson River to see the falcons. They made their way around to the western deck and squeezed themselves against the railing in among the huddled tourists.

They peered over one of the rounded limestone pillars that broke the sharp fall way down to the street below. Adam didn't seem scared at all, to Alice's surprise. She felt so dizzy that she wondered if she could stand it. She pushed her knees into the pillar and fixed her gaze on the horizon. Planes drove across the skyline and, one after the other, serenely headed down towards Newark's runways. Cruise ships, sailboats, and barges cut along the Hudson, flat as a long stretch of grey packing tape. Helicopters hovered above the island, their rotors spinning like beanie propellers. The activity was lulling. She was lost in a vision of a possible nocturne of the Hudson, something of a cross between the inscrutable grandeur of a Thomas Cole and the haunted eye of Albert Pinkham Ryder, who drew the eerie landscape up close no matter how far away it was. The contemplation of those silvery dark waters would provide the drama in her picture, Alice reflected, then felt a yanking at her sleeve. Adam had been trying to get her attention for at least 3 minutes, he said! His gaze was darting about as he scanned the sky intently, settling finally upon Alice and, sensing her presence again, shared the object of his agitation, which bordered on sheer betrayal.

"There are no birds!"

Glancing back up at the sky, Emma marveled at the view as if it were the very first time she laid her eyes on the Empire State Building blooming outside the living room window. It was this scene that decided Luke on the apartment, minutes after the real estate agent led them into the room. A 15-foot glass span covered most of the wall. Manhattan stretched out before them to the north, with the Empire State and Chrysler Buildings posed above the skyline like an imperial couple holding court. Luke reached for Emma's hand and drew her to the perch, where they remained, lost in a daydream of themselves in that light. The agent was not one to schedule daydreams into her calendar, and no sooner did she clear her throat impatiently to get on with the tour than Luke turned to her and said they would take it. Emma blushed deeply. Surprised but pleased, the agent insisted they at least look around. The three rooms cost more than they could afford, but from that day forward they never missed the rent, even during the recession, which was something they took pride in. Times were tough, and getting tougher, and gazing was a precious commodity. Home was that window into which a thousand cropped skies accompanied Emma's thoughts, where a faint reminder of humanity lit up TV screens during her fits of insomnia. Turning her gaze upward toward the darkening skies, her eyes would bath in the glow of blues, reds, purples, and whites stacked pyramid-like atop the massive grey deco building in the distance.

Now looking at the Tower in search of Adam and Alice, she was frankly sick. She imagined herself with them on the Observation Deck surrounded only by thin air, which would somehow grab hold of her and pull her into the void. The empty clutches beyond the rootless edge of things was intolerable, even in her imagination. As she strained impossibly into the twilight, the spire burst into bright-lime green and floodlights drenched the building's top in blue and purple. With it, fear changed to awe: she felt herself drenched in color and wondered if it poured over her son on the deck. The fact that she could have this thought about her son, or rather the fact that she even had a son never lost its mystery: there was a person both of her and unto himself, and who was now miles up, on a legendary rooftop, looking at birds. She imagined the look of wonder in his black eyes as he beheld the raptors racing around the spire, then plunging ravenous into the depths of their nocturnal hunt. She turned away, instinctually, to let him go, at least momentarily.

Adam was beholding nothing, or at least no birds, but was encouraged by the darkening skies when Andie told him they might be there. Holding Alice's hand he made a slow promenade around the deck. By now, the sun had dipped below the horizon, and the city flickered with street lamps and headlights, followed by millions of windows that blinked yellowy white here and there as if the Island were awakening from a stupor. Adam loved the dazzle, above and below, and wondered if he and his dad could pitch a tent up there. They would be so close to the planets—maybe see Venus or Mars! But as the last lights left the sky on their third circle around the deck, he felt increasingly despondent. There simply were no birds. He looked up at Alice tearfully and she took him in her arms. He snuggled into her shoulder, tired and chilled from the disappointment. As he looked wistfully out at the moon, just past the spire, there was a sudden flutter of black wings right near him—and then it vanished! Adam jumped down from Alice's arms and ran off, peering over the edge here and there as Alice ran after him, calling to him to come back by her side.

"But we have to see it *again!*"

"See *what*? Did you see a bird?"

"I don't know what it was—maybe the shadow of a bird gone crazy."

Out of the corner of his eye he caught the flutter once again and darted towards it. Alice saw it too and rubbed her eyes. *It couldn't be.* She glanced up at the full moon.

"Adam, I think it's a bat!"

"A bat? It can't be a bat! There are no caves up here!"

"I could swear it was a bat. Let's look around again."

They walked around the deck, surreptitiously this time, glancing here and there, just like spies, Adam thought. As they made their way to the western side of the deck, Adam began to doubt he had seen anything at all. He grew more tired and unsure as the skies finished darkening into a black pitch. Alice reassured him that she'd seen it too, but couldn't figure out where it had gone.

"There it is!" a kindly voice called to them. A tall man with an eager smile motioned them his way. Adam saw his scope and ran over to him.

"Are you an astronomer?"

"No," he laughed. "I'm a naturalist. And that flying creature you saw was indeed a bat. When the wind changed course, I didn't think I'd see anything up here tonight, but little did I know I'd find one of those guys!"

"So it *is* a bat! How'd it get way up here?"

"Well, it's not that surprising, I suppose. They come out at twilight and can fly quite high. Maybe we'll be lucky and see him again. I'm Michael, by the way."

"I'm Adam, and this is Alice. Do you come up here all the time?"

"I actually live in Maine. I'm down here for a conference. I thought this would be a good place for bird watching, especially now that they're beginning to migrate back north."

"You live in Maine? But we go there every summer, to Acadia!" Michael was quiet for a moment, peering into his scope, while the child danced around him, eager to continue their conversation.

"But how do the birds know it's time to migrate? Who decides? How does it work?"

Fortunately, birds were Michael's specialty; he had even been writing a book about the birds of Acadia for the last few years. He was currently preparing a chapter on migration, so Adam's question was at the forefront of his thoughts. He was even considering writing a second book on the subject for children. Come to think of it, maybe he would have a character like Adam ask these sorts of questions. What he didn't know was that Adam was rarely satisfied by an answer. He looked down at the inquisitive fellow, eager to help him understand: "Well, some of them will stay in the city, but most of them migrate back north."

"But why? What happens to them in the spring? How do they know it's getting warmer where they come from? And they're so far away from home, hundreds or thousands of miles! How do they find their way back?"

Michael was amused but also touched by the curiosity of the child. "Birds migrate along something called a flyway. It is the route that they take, either along the coastline, a mountain range, or even a river. The thing is, the route they take south is not always the route they take back north."

"Well, the bus route I take to go to school is different than the one I take back home. When it's time to go, the bus monitor comes to my classroom to get the bus kids. But how do the birds know?"

"The best I can say is that *they just know.*"

"But *how*? How does a bird *know* something?"

"It is in their genes. They're born *knowing* to migrate. They know when to go south, in the fall, and when to go north, in the spring. They know their time."

"I don't really think that answers the question."

"Why not?"

"I don't know what genes are, but it has to be more than being born a certain way. I mean, maybe a lot of the birds migrate because they love their homes and just want to go back, right?" Adam asked intently.

"Well, yes, that's true. They get attached to their homes, just like we do. But migration also depends on other factors, like where they can get the most food in the winter. Like the birds, I think we are born knowing things. We just don't pay enough attention to them."

Alice had been staring out at the horizon, deep in thought. "Birds know their time," she murmured.

"Come look, Adam, quick!" Michael called.

I saw it, I saw it, I saw an actual bat! On top of the Empire State Building! I can't believe it, Adam thought with pride. By the time Alice looked into the scope the bat was gone. Adam was jumping up and down, his cheeks pink with the wind. She took the child by the hand. He glowed all the more under the light of the moon, which was practically full. Then his face burst into a giant yawn.

"Looks like somebody's tired!" Michael noted warmly. "Here, take my card. Look me up when you come to Maine again. I live on Mt. Desert Island."

"Really? Wait till Mama hears about this! I hope we can see some falcons because there sure aren't any up here," Adam added sadly.

"Oh, there are lots of them, and in the summer you'll see the fledglings learn how to fly off the cliffs of Champlain Mountain."

"We pass that mountain every five seconds! Boy, am I glad we met you; I had no idea birds were learning to fly there. But one last thing: are you *sure* that was a bat?"

"Absolutely. I've been studying flying creatures for the past twenty years, and that was no bird. In fact, I'm quite sure it was a Little Brown Bat, out hunting moths."

"What? There are moths way up here?" Alice exclaimed, who was becoming more keenly interested in flying creatures as the conversation went on.

"Yes, and believe it or not, moths migrate, too. And they fly even higher than the Empire State Building, always on the lookout to catch a ride on the wind," Michael explained.

"How long would it take me to know everything, like you?" Adam asked, looking earnestly into his eyes. There seemed to be thousands of amazing things that happened every minute in the world.

Michael was struck by how much this city boy wanted to talk about birds and bats in this kind of detail. "Just remember how lucky you are that you saw the Little Brown Bat. They're dying by the thousands from white-nose syndrome. Someday they might even become extinct."

Adam didn't like the idea of anything disappearing, and he felt sad for the bats but was also troubled by them. "But aren't they dangerous? I think there are vampire bats that come out on Halloween... Can they actually suck our blood, like Dracula?" He looked off to the moon, and his mouth went dry imagining those creatures of the darkness.

"Dracula is just a story. People cannot turn into bats! That's a rotten myth that's given bats a bad name. I know they look weird and scary, but they are actually very gentle. Yes, it's true: bats are one of our greatest creature friends. They eat tons of insects and pollinate the plants—"

"What? I thought bees did that..."

"Well, bats do it, too. Funny thing, there's actually a Bumblebee Bat. It's so small; its wingspan is just six inches."

Picturing the Bumblebee Bat, Adam thought there wouldn't be a better costume for Halloween; he would have to tell his mother so she could make it for him. He hugged Michael goodbye, sure that they would meet again in Acadia. Alice steered him toward the exit, where he turned to glance up at the spire that glowed emerald green through ascending panes, like the stained glass he once saw in a country church when his family went to Vermont. Back down on the sidewalk, he looked up one last time at the towering skyscraper where a lone Brown Bat was on his nightly hunt. Bats were his friends, and he didn't even know it. He made an audible sigh of relief and strode on with confidence.

He looked up at Alice, who seemed far away even though she was by his side and holding his hand as tightly as usual.

"What do you wish you were?" he asked, to bring her back.

She smiled at him wistfully. "I suppose I wish I were a bird."

"So you could fly way up to the Empire State Building and swoop down again as fast as lightning?"

"Well... what I'd like even better is to migrate."

"You mean like the falcons?"

"And the robins, and the hawks, and the swallows, and the ducks, and the geese—"

"—and the bats and the butterflies!" he chimed in as they made their way toward the bright green bulb of the 6 line, then hurried down the stairs for the arriving train. As they sped through the dark tunnel, he reached for her hand and held it in silence all the way home.

"We never did figure it out, Dad," said Adam as they made their way through Washington Square.

"What's that, Adam?"

"Why the falcons aren't scared of those big eagles on the Chrysler Building."

"I know. I'm working on it. But I bet you have an idea about it, huh?"

"Yeah. I think they're trying to get over something so they'll feel strong."

"But falcons are strong already, no?"

"Maybe they don't know how strong they really are if they can also be scared of something."

As they passed the playground, Luke noticed that Adam didn't ask to go in. For the first time, the playground didn't matter. Luke smiled warmly at Adam, who looked back with a serious face as he wanted to continue the discussion.

"I mean, when you're afraid, it makes things hard. And maybe the falcons wanted to feel free, so they decided to make their nest right under the gargoyle's nose. I bet Mama gets scared sometimes, too. But, were *you* ever afraid of anything, Dad?"

Luke's heart skipped a beat. There were many things that had scared him as a child and others that scared him now, but it seemed pointless to talk about them with his son, who suddenly seemed so bold, preferring to encourage that feeling in his child.

"The only thing I'm afraid of is that I won't finish my play on time!"

"But that's easy! You're good at telling stories. You just have to think of the ending."

"The ending, my young Jedi friend, is the hardest part!"

"Maybe because you like the story so much you don't want it to end. But isn't that good?" he asked, scanning his father's face for the quiet smile that was such a comfort to the child; and the smile then appeared.

Adam had a way of saying just the right thing, and Luke, so preoccupied and often tormented, took solace in his company. There were few other people in the world, if any, who had this effect on him. Luke felt lighter and quite proud of the little fellow.

Adam continued his walk with a sense of relief. It wouldn't be so bad to grow up after all. Grown-ups' problems were so much easier than kid problems! To prolong their outing, Adam dove into some bushes, beyond his father's reach, and crawled out the other way, where his eye seized upon a glowing piece of sunray poking up from under a clump of withered maple leaves. He knelt beside it and cleared the leaves away, uncovering a cluster of small daffodils. Adam couldn't believe how yellow the petals were, so bright against the remains of winter. The first flowers of spring! He looked around for others that would need his help, brushing aside a lot of twigs and leaves. He found more buds just at the point of bloom. *I'll have to come back tomorrow to see if they've opened!* He thought of Mama's happy face and decided he would let her in on it.

He watched a robin hopping by, then wondered why it stopped. What was it looking at? And why did he have his head cocked to one side? Did he hear something? Suddenly the robin pecked the earth, then yanked out a long wriggling worm. Adam laughed. Now that the snow was gone, he was glad to see that there was so much to do, like look at bugs, and flowers, and birds. These robins sure were clever. They could hear worms in the ground! He put his ear to the dirt but heard nothing, then wondered if the robins were just back from migrating and where they'd been all winter. He didn't remember seeing any robins during his snowball fights with his dad, only some cardinals, redder than red against the snowy drifts in the courtyard. Maybe the robins hid in the trees during the winter months. He'd have to re-member to ask Michael about it in the summer. The falcons were exciting, but there was probably a lot to learn from the birds that stayed home all year-round. Migration was pretty risky after all—those birds might never come back. Adam sighed and walked back toward the path where his father was calling him.

III. Emma

April was covered with mud. Thunderstorms kept roaring through the city; on a good day, it drizzled all day. But unless there were walls of rain or bolts of lightning, Emma would not miss the unfolding of spring. But it was irritating. Slogging in rain gear through the hills of Central Park felt almost like mud season in Maine. Whenever Emma dreamed of living in Acadia, she remembered her visit a few years earlier, just when the snow and ice had started thawing. The earth roiled constantly, dark and oozing. Off on a trail, just moments after touchdown in Bar Harbor, she sank knee-deep in a mud pit. She would have laughed had it been summer, when, soaked with a warm rain, she could barely tear herself away from the forest. But thawing earth was different; it was weirdly sticky, clay-like, clammy, and unimaginably cold. April was just better in Manhattan, she concluded, and decided to make the most of it.

Meandering along the fringes of the Ramble, she stopped to admire a clump of hellebores. Here were the last of them, sheltered between a boulder and a rotting tree stump. Emma had first noticed hellebores on a frozen day in January, at first thinking they were frost flowers that the wet wind had imprinted on the snow. But they were real and bold. Throughout her wintry jaunts, she looked at them with uncertain awe at how they hung on to the very last, unlike other petals, which all dropped when they'd withered. She stooped to clear away a mass of leaves and twigs, heavy with rain, to see if there were any bugs or worms crawling about in the melted mud. The deep brown soil was surprisingly gritty and claylike; she took off her glove to squish some between her fingers. As the springtime earth dripped off her hand, it left a sandy reddish stain, glistening here and there as if it had bits of copper in it. She pulled off the other glove, thrust both hands into the earth and dug up to her elbows. She paused to observe the changing hues of the ground: brown, then reddish-brown beneath it. She then worked her way further down, plunging her arms as deep as they would go; and then, thoroughly prone, with one cheek pressed against the forest floor, she pulled out her right hand, covered in black muck.

Struck by those variations in the soil, she stood up and wiped herself off. She then left the park, returning with stacks of containers she purchased at a hardware store and a shovel borrowed from a helpful gardener in the Ramble. As much as she liked getting dirty, she was grateful for the digging tool. She spent the rest of the day collecting samples, digging into the different layers that the rains had made pliable, her work halted only by the chill and falling dusk. Finding refuge in the yellowy beam of a soulful lamppost, she clutched her pencil with muddy fingers and on a small pad noted the diverse elements of the soil—or at least what she could make out with the naked eye—that she had scrawled on the specimen lids with chalk, smudging now in the misty hour and risking an ephemeral fate. Emma indicated the approximate site of each dig, using a code lifted from a nearby lamppost. Throughout the Park, there were over a thousand of those cast iron fireflies, which, while lighting up the night for solitary wanderers and romantic couples, also served a crucial navigational purpose for Emma the explorer. A code imprinted near the base translated her location—the first two numbers referring to the nearest street, and the second two denoting either West Side (odd numbers) or East Side (even numbers). To this she added her own code to note the area—Ramble, Great Meadow, Reservoir, etc. — and as well, the soil's color, texture, and possible minerals, fungi and whatever else she noticed. Of course, in the rain-soaked earth, there was considerable seepage between layers, but the glistening water emphasized the multiple variations of hues and tones that would not have been visible if the earth were dry. She sought to amass as many soil samples as possible, both in color and texture, roaming the woods, pond fringes, meadows, and walkways of Central Park for her collection.

On her way out of the park, she thought about those soil samples and how compelling it was to classify them; but then it came to her, quite suddenly, that she could use the soil directly in her work, and that she might actually water-color with the rain-dripped cakes of earth. On the subway ride home, she pondered how she might apply those earthy tones to paper. She might need some sort of base, or could mix up bits of mud with chalk or paint. Having used nothing but pencil for the last ten years she felt uncertain about abandoning the medium that had so closely caught the spirit of her work. But by the time she walked the last block home she was ready to experiment, figuring that maybe she wouldn't need her pencils at all, which for Emma was a radical idea.

Adam and Luke were used to seeing Emma come home with her hair full of leaves and twigs, but her muddy face today surprised them. She saw herself in their wide eyes and looked in the hall mirror. She liked her metamorphosis, sensing how this new adventure had taken hold of her. She put down her bag and proceeded to strip off her earth-caked boots and slicker. Her cheeks were red with the evening chill—too cold to kiss, thought Adam as he pulled back from her icy face. He peered into her bag, hoping for surprises, but only found container after container with nothing but a bunch of dirt in it. Emma scooped them up and took them into her studio, where she examined each one quickly under the light, her mind moving rapidly. She couldn't wait to be alone with them and all that mud.

Hours later, eyes heavy, she slipped out of bed. Despite her exhaustion, she could not find sleep, continuing to roam and dig, and lay awake. Furtively, she headed for her studio, careful not to wake the others, and grinned as if she were stealing through the ethereal night with an altogether earthly visitor, the incomparable Mud Man. She tiptoed past Adam's room, her heart pounding as she crept into her studio and closed herself in. She proceeded to transfer the mud samples into glass jars so she could study them more closely. Some of them, nearly dry, had lost their rainy luster. How might she retain it or re-create it? She looked in her storage closet for some heavy watercolor paper and found an unused block way back on the top shelf, covered with a film of dust. Could she paint with the mud? How much of it would the paper hold? She would need some kind of medium to fix it to the paper ground. She was worried about using paste; all she had was Elmer's and it would make the dirt too milky. Rubber cement? Too thick, too much character. Besides, it was toxic and would probably damage the paper. Instinctively, she went into the kitchen. Oatmeal? Ridiculous. Flour? Too pasty. She thought she might use tempera after all but decided against it; she wanted the binder to yield the mud in its natural form, to the extent possible, and ready-made tempera combined eggs with a pre-selected pigment. She would make her own egg mixture with the earth colors she had dug up, and would also try combinations that yielded varying degrees of opacity.

It was near dawn when she studied the results, comparing countless thick brush strokes, some taking up at least half a page. There were those, as they had dried, that left gaps between dirt particles, while others were shiny but stringy, like chewed or spit-up bits of yarn. But the batch of dirt mixed with yolk, rather than egg whites, maintained a consistent muddiness throughout the whole stroke, and revealed the natural metallic substance in the soil without the distracting sheen that came from the albumen. There was a problem, though: the yolk gave the mud a slightly yellow hue, creating a sepia effect, only worse, as if some stray animal had peed on it. But she did not give up on using eggs, deciding to wait a few days to see how time might change the color and texture of the different combinations. She set her pages on a high rack for further study.

A week later she went back to examine the results. As she held the paper to the sunlight, her dirt-and-water mixture drifted off the page, leaving nothing but some sandy particles. She was also disappointed in the dirt-and-egg-white mixture, which had far less substance than when she applied it with the brush. But the yolk/mud blend held firm, with twigs and dirt clumps texturing the ground of the paper, and, fortunately, the sepia effect had attenuated. As she set it down on her worktable to look at it under the gentle desk light, she froze—the yolky blotch revealed a footprint, as if some stealthy ghost had stepped there and then sped away on hearing Emma turn the doorknob. "That's it," she murmured to the room. She would make footprints—*underground footprints*, whose hue and texture would change the deeper they sank into the earth. *She would go hiking underground.*

All that month, Adam and Luke watched Emma come and go with containers, first empty and then full of mud. She would spend days in the furthest reaches of the boroughs, wading through brackish water and salt marshes in Jamaica Bay, where the mud was particularly nutrient-rich; she climbed the hills of Fort Tryon and roamed the fields in Van Cortlandt Park. She would bring back smells of salt and clay, and a profuse variety of soil, with different textures, colors and consistencies (and many dozens of eggs). She worked for hours trying to figure out the best way to bind the dirt to the paper, making hundreds of mud swatches with gum Arabic and Mod Podge and other substances. Her studio floor was tracked all over with dirt spills and heel and toe prints, and had a faint smell of breakfast.

The house was permanently strewn with twigs and leaves and dirt. Luke joked that deer would soon be grazing around the dining room table. Adam dreamt one night that a tree was growing in the apartment and wasn't sure if that was a good thing. Emma, too, was troubled. She had always brought the things of nature into her studio for further study, but using mud instead of pencil lent her work an altogether different materiality. And that made her uneasy. There had always been this foundational boundary, faint at times but always palpable, between art and nature. Pencil tended to stay in the realm of evocation; it could even render violence without transgression. With mud, there might be a loss of lightness. She knew that pigments were made from minerals, but painting with actual mud felt like an intrusion; it was too close to the thing itself, creating an intimacy that made her a little nauseated, as if she were bringing a plodding heaviness of raw reality into a handmade world; it was simply contrary to her sensibility. And yet she didn't want to, couldn't, stop. She felt a looming, as she often did in those hours before dawn, when things in the apartment took on a dream life, as if the laws of gravity did not quite hold them. But now the air was shaped into the form of a trail, with all the character of descent, through the forest, absolutely *into* the forest, down into its very floor. What was this imperative to go into the earth? And *how far* down? The cool air in a burrowed tunnel, the slight give of the ground, roots jutting down from the earth's ceiling, an underground clearing up ahead, a faint light cast by a random passage to the surface, all flickered through her meditations.

She did some quick sketches then turned her attention to the jar of dirt on her worktable. She remained there for some time, quite still, staring into it as if it were some dark crystal ball, until an incongruous rush of migrating birds just beyond the window broke the silence with their landing calls— the warblers, whose impossible pitches sounded exactly like bright yellow, mingling with the *chip-chip-burr* of the Red Tanager. Was this home, or just a stopping-place along the Atlantic flyway? She remembered Audubon's *Scarlet Tanager*, took a book, his *Birds of America,* from the shelf, and marveled at the textured feathers.

Her search had something to do with spring, with the thawing and churning, the wriggling earthworms wrestling with the soil, heads and tails flailing up now and then out of the ground, naked, clean with slime and pinkish grey and disappearing as they slipped away. One could catch a faint glimpse of the multiple rings that spiraled down their bodies. Emma, too, wanted to wrestle with the surface, to see how life below could push itself out. Could one exist down there, as if it were a common thing to walk underground? If so, pencil would fall short here, because texture would now be a necessity. The footprint she had in mind would not be the object of her dirt painting but, rather, the trace of a wandering in the earth. She reflected on the problem of illumination, as there was no light source underground. How would she move along the tunnel-like trail? There might be faint cracks in the surface through which some quiet light might stream... Her work often wrestled with such problems, but the solutions would be different now since she was no longer drawing. To what end this earth narrative anyway except that it helped her lean further into her painting, if one could call it that. And then, how might she capture gradations of light with this gouache-like mud? She turned to Audubon's *Magnificent Frigatebird,* and looked carefully at its richness of shadowy blacks and greys that textured the plumage as the bird plunged downward towards the edge of the page. The painting offered some clues to how she would work through the challenge. She was fascinated by the fact that the grey plumage owed some of its richness to graphite. Perhaps she could mingle her pencils after all. She paused at Audubon's description of the Frigatebird, "a very beautiful old male in spring plumage." Emma was sensitive to its dignity and to the way the deep grey feathers seemed rather like a bark cutout, with patterned fissures, ever so delicate.

She opened the set of pastels that Luke had given her for her birthday a year ago when she'd been sure that she would never use them, and took some big pieces of sidewalk chalk off a shelf in Adam's room. She laid the chalk and the pastels next to the cakes of brown, white, and black watercolor, then placed various soil clumps on individual trays; and so she then set to work, building up layers with multiple washes, then applying darker shades of pastel over light ones, wetting the sticks now and again as she went along, their traces reminding her of moist dirt. Thus she seemed to capture some of the density she desired, scraping a bit here and there, filling the gaps with strokes of mud. It wasn't as hard as she thought: she could create relief and even impose a semblance of layers of earth, albeit in a highly condensed manner. Some eight hours later, by the time she heard Adam's eager voice and ran from her studio to greet him and the new day, she had left behind—faint yet distinct—a footprint.

Later that morning, Emma returned to her studio to look at her work, with Adam trailing behind her. He peered over the edge of her worktable. There was dirt everywhere and a ton of things he wasn't used to seeing, including his chalk! What was she doing? Mama always loved to draw leaves and bark, fruit and vegetables in a special way. But this was not a drawing. He wasn't sure exactly what it was.

"It's a painting, Adam."

"Why isn't it hanging up like your drawings? Is it too heavy?"

"It is heavier than my drawings, but that's not the problem. I don't want to hang it because I don't want people to be thinking about a wall when they look at it."

"So will it be on the ceiling looking down at me?"

Emma laughed. "No, just the opposite. It'll lie flat."

"On the floor? What if someone steps on it? Wait! It looks like someone already has!"

"Well, yes, except that someone did not step *on* it but kind of hiked through it."

"You mean like the man taking a bite out of the painting?"

It took her a moment to grasp his meaning.

"You mean the *Painting Bitten by a Man* that we saw at the Museum of Modern Art?"

"That's my favorite, except for the ones with Greek gods," he said, remembering his beloved mythology book. "I like those best of all. But who do you think bit it, Mama, because it really did look like teeth marks."

"They say it was the artist himself, Jasper Johns."

"I don't think it was... why would he say *bitten by a man* if it was himself? A *Man* is somebody else! If he bit it, he would have said *Painting Bitten by Me*."

"But that's exactly the point, Adam. The artist makes a drawing or a painting, and wants it to be about somebody who's not himself. What I mean is, he wants to change the way people look at things, as if one of us walking by the canvas stopped and thought, *wow, this looks delicious* and sank their teeth into it."

"I hope your painting won't be called *Painting Hiked in by a Woman* because I'll know it was you all along, and I don't think you should lie about it."

"Well, that would be a very serious accusation, and I will remember it when I decide on a title."

"But why did Jasper bite the painting anyway?"

"Maybe he wanted to be *in* it. That's how I feel about this mud." Adam had a point, she reflected. It makes sense to hike through dirt; feet and soil go together, but eating and oil paint don't, and that's what probably made the Johns painting so compelling. It wasn't meant to be, and yet it *was*.

A faint smell of early rain lingered in the breeze drifting through the studio window. Adam lay down on the couch and thought about whether he would be an artist someday, and the kinds of things he might do, like make birds really fly in the painting's sky or bugs crawl in a garden. He thought of the millipede he discovered on a walk with his grandparents a few summers ago. He stooped to pick it up and laughed at the tickling of the hundreds of tiny legs crawling slowly across his hand. He fed it a leaf and watched it chew its way through. Why would anybody make a painting when they could just sit with a real bug in their hand? Jasper must've been sad that morning when he bit his painting, all alone and no one to eat with. Adam gazed at the window, watching the gentle movements of the billowing curtain. It looked alive to him, dancing in the sunlight, touching down for a moment on the sill till it drew back, then further back, tense for a long second, then pushed forth into the air, as if it were on a swing. That's what it was, a girl on a swing, a girl dressed in white. Adam scrambled to his feet with a sudden recollection. Glancing back at his mother's painting, he exclaimed, "I sure hope it won't be muddy out, today of all days!"

"And why is that?"

"Don't you remember? We're going on a picnic with Alice!"

They were headed along Eastern Parkway toward the main entrance to the Brooklyn Botanical Gardens, Emma walking briskly, with Adam bouncing by her side. He didn't get what the big deal was and why they had to go exactly when the lilacs were in bloom. He wasn't sure what a lilac was, but it sounded like an old-fashioned aunt he had to visit. In any event, the lilacs had postponed their picnic, so he didn't really want to look at them. But as soon as he spotted the gated entrance at the end of the block, his heart began to quicken in hopes of seeing Alice who might be searching for him and his Mama that very minute.

Alice was indeed heading for the main entrance but was out of sight around the corner on Flatbush Avenue. Her gait was slowed by the thought preoccupying her of an altogether different park: Sequoia and Kings Canyon in California. An odd sequence of events had taken her to that place way out West, starting back on that December night in Washington Square, when she had climbed the great old elm. Once back on the ground, she had found herself disoriented. She almost got lost on the way back to Battery Park and, scared by the feeling, started to rush, then run, to get back home. But a part of her was left behind up there in the tree; she began to doubt she would ever truly come down from those crooked branches. She soon made it back, entering breathless, and regained herself momentarily, finding her perch on the makeshift window seat in her living room. But she soon drew away from the hollow Trade Center site below.

She took refuge in some landscapes on an Internet museum site—jumping to Corot, whose work moved her like no one else's. Whether in pencil, charcoal, or oil, there was such understated passion in his precision; leaves, branches, stumps and meadows always seemed to just *appear*, as if emerging straight out of his reverie as he looked at the world. In his work, there was no greater mystery than the tree, Alice reflected, marveling at the dominance of his oaks, his chestnut trees, and other trees harder to identify. How strangely *bold* they were. Gnarled trunks in the forest were caught here and there by a gentle light, as dead limbs leaned and cut through the air over tangled bushes. Corot's trees were the great inhabitants of the Morvan, Normandy, the outskirts of Paris, and the Italian lakes. As Alice clicked and scrolled through the site, she thought about what had preoccupied her ever since she first began to paint, and wander: the landscape.

She clicked into some works by Moran, which caught her by surprise: she wasn't expecting such beauty. She thought back to the retrospective at the National Gallery, where she had gone with her family years before to see his oils and watercolors of the American West. She was just a child and very taken with those pictures. She remembered skipping through the miles of soft pink boulders, gigantic skies billowing with mist, gushing rivers breaking through gorges, huge cliffs and mountains that dwarfed the Indians below. Steeply above, pink clouds opened into what might have been heaven. '*What is this place?*' she wondered aloud. Her mother explained that these were the very first images of the famous Rocky and Colorado mountain ranges and the great Grand Canyon of the West. President Grant found those sights so beautiful and pure that they inspired him to create the world's very first National Park, a kind of natural wonderland. *Well, that was something,* thought the child. *This man Moran was the first to imagine the West before anybody else. He actually made up paintings that became real parks.* As they toured the Gallery, Jenna read to her about the different expeditions that Moran had joined; but Alice wasn't listening to most of it. She wondered, instead, if different people had different eyes, and different views of the same thing, and what her own view might look like. In the gift shop she chose a poster of *An Arizona Sunset Near the Grand Canyon,* and for years would gaze into its roiling sky and wonder if it really was on fire.

Much had changed since then; those paintings now seemed too bombastic for her taste, except for some of the watercolors that, while akin to Turner in the use of light, reminded her more of Cezanne, in the way a singular mountain could loom and hold the landscape. But this East Hampton series had a completely different feel. The *June East Hampton* paintings were on a scale less swollen than the works of the Great West, and yet they caught the windblown season in full bloom. Aside from Corot, Alice thought she had never seen trees so thoroughly alive, whether crowding richly at the forest's edge or figuring dreamlike beneath the cloudy sky as if its mere reflection. The lone tree in *East Moriches* stood its ground so courageously below the passing storm clouds; its dark fist of limbs and leaves seemed an earthly answer to the light-burst hole in the grey clouds above. The two great blotches similar in shape and size created negative and positive space—but which was which? What looked like a majestic oak near the shoreline was overcome by the darkness that rode completely up its trunk and down again, spreading like a hooped skirt over the grasses below. The encroached darkness threatened to transform the tree altogether into a wicked black blotch were it not for the soft green leaves in the outer crown. The bulbous cloud of white light, bursting out of the darkened sky in the background, broke the canvas, and the gaze, in two, with the left eye drawn to the cloud-light and the right eye to the tree-shadow. The effect was so powerful that it seemed to obliterate foreground and background, despite the tiny windmill in the distance. The more Alice looked at the painting, the more she felt like she *was* that tree, looking into the sky.

She spent the week at the Brooklyn Museum of Art roaming the collection of American Landscapes. Until that moment, she felt that she had never quite understood the paintings of Kensett, finding herself inexorably drawn into their vanishing point, alive to the quiet luminosity in those seamless strokes of boulders, skies and waters. She came upon Bierstadt and was captivated by *A Storm in the Rocky Mountains, Mt. Rosalie*, from 1866, and the way sweeping, broken hoops of darkness and light were strewn across the canvas. Before he went out west, Bierstadt had observed Union troops up close and in battle. While there was no bloodshed in his paintings of the Civil War, Alice knew that he had witnessed violence. In *Guerrilla Warfare*, rifles joined to shoulder and hip sockets were extensions of the Union soldiers' pointed gaze, the muzzle directing the viewer straight to Confederates across fields blanched by the pallor of the off-white sky. She wondered if the spiritual intensity of the snow-capped Mt. Rosalie, looming in the cloudy heaven of the Rockies, emerged somehow from Bierstadt's attempt to recover from the War.

Back home she roamed the West on the Internet, where she came across a park ranger's account of having spent the night listening to the rapids tumbling from the Upper Falls into the great gorge in the Canyon. She then spent weeks reading anecdotes of rangers from across the country, and wading through employment sites for the National Parks Service. *Just me and the trees...*

Turning the corner onto Eastern Parkway, she was roused by Adam calling to her from the entrance to the Gardens. She ran toward him, biting her lip, and scooped him up in her arms. They passed through the garden gates with Emma close behind.

"Woooooooow," yelled Adam, when he saw the emerald lawn that stretched before him and dashed ahead like a dog let loose, zigzagging across the grass, crouching behind bushes to hide from Alice then bursting out again as she ran up to find him. He frolicked to his heart's content, then paused for a moment on a bench, breathless yet eager to play again. He tried to call to her in a whisper, but she was already down at the other end of the lawn admiring the fountain; but, to his surprise, she turned toward him as if she'd heard him anyway, so he whispered a few words of nonsense, to see if she heard those.

"What did I say?" he demanded, grinning when she finally made it to his side.

"Fish troll, lollipop, and boing-boing!" Alice repeated.

"Whisper something to me!" he shouted, running to the other end of the lawn.

"I will always love you," she whispered his way.

"Say something funny!" He called back to her, smiling from ear to ear. And so they whispered to each other from across the Osborne Garden, jokes and silly secrets, marveling at their ability to communicate like spies, until Adam realized that, if Alice could hear him, so could everybody else. He broke into a crazy dance, then rolled and tumbled. Tired out at last, he pulled Alice down with him into the freshly mown grass, and the two lay on their backs, Adam kicking off his sandals.

Bordered by flowering walls and pergolas crowned with vines of the palest purple wisteria, perfect azaleas, and fiery teacup tulips, this entranceway to the Brooklyn Botanical Garden was intensely alive for Emma as she stood in it, just before she spotted Adam and Alice lolling on the green, their bare toes pointing up at the gigantic May sky. She came over and lay down beside them and got into a playful argument with Adam about which animals were in the clouds above them. He was sure there was an eagle flying with a fish in its beak, while Emma saw a kangaroo with a Joey in its pouch. He couldn't believe that that's what they called baby kangaroos.

"Is there a baby animal called an Adam?" he asked, sure that he had finally stumped his mother.

"Yes, there is, and—it's YOU!"

He laughed and threw himself upon her, and she would've stayed but for the calling of the lilacs just below the fountain. Alice, sensing Emma's interest in those flowers and eager to please, was on her feet in an instant, but Adam took off the other way, eager for more hide-and-seek.

Deep in the clutches of their wafting scent, Emma moved toward the stone staircase that led down to the lilac meadow. If ever a flower was all-American, it was the lilac, the back-yard favorite of gardeners, the tree-like bushes aging well for centuries. Wasn't the tallest one called President Lincoln? The lilac was Emma's most beloved flower; its scent meant spring and the springtime of childhood. The droopy purple buds bordered the beds of her father's garden. He had made those beds with his own hands and planted the lilacs the year she was born. The year she turned 4, in the hush of early May, Emma tiptoed gingerly across an imaginary tightrope to the bushes that had lain dormant until then. But what a year that was! She had never seen her father so happy and would always eagerly accompany him on his backyard stroll, year after year, waiting for that delighted smile of his when he saw the first lilac buds. As they grew taller, they sheltered her like castle walls. She would play behind them with many a made-up friend and foe, until one day, in a fit of anger, she ran away from home behind those very lilacs. She filled her pillowcase with her stuffed animals and a box of cereal and waited furiously for what seemed like forever. Finally, she heard her mother call her name repeatedly throughout the house, then out in the garden. Sure at last that she was truly missed, she skipped back out across the lawn to greet her mother—who hadn't even noticed that she'd run away!

From the stone stairway leading to the lilacs, Emma watched Alice and Adam play a few rounds of *statues*, a game they had made up last summer. They would take turns holding the other's hand, swing wildly, then let go; and, as unexpectedly as possible, the swinger would yell "freeze!" and order the other to become some historical figure, god, or beast, depending on what the pose inspired. Adam was now strutting around like the furious Giant atop the beanstalk, and Alice joined in by creeping away from him with a golden egg under her arm. At the end of the round, they made their way over to Emma, and the three of them lingered there, taking in the view of the billowing patch of world below.

The lavender froth of waves streaked with white, blue, and magenta splashed petal-like droplets of blooms into the wind; the air was filled with the scents of purple soda and fresh white linen. Adam ran down to the meadow and was soon bobbing his head among the bushes, comparing the smells and colors of the different blooms. Emma ran down to join him, giddy with the beauty of it all and led the others to the center of the triangular garden. They made their home beneath an archway of blooms until Adam spotted a bunny and ran after it down the lawn. Alice started running after him, then paused, taking a blanket from her bag, and unfolded it beneath a maple tree. Might they sit for a moment, just where they were? Adam jumped onto the blanket playfully, then glanced up at her, startled by the silence that ensued. At first, Emma thought that Alice wanted to do some sketching, but the girl's sad face said otherwise. She clearly had something to tell them.

"I got a job!" she blurted out.

"That's wonderful! What are you going to do?" Emma was impressed that her student had found something so quickly, in the midst of a recession no less. Adam looked on, feeling not at all impressed, with a kind of worry fluttering across his face.

"But I'll see you at night?" he asked Alice.

"I'm afraid not, Adam," she said solemnly. "My job is taking me far away."

"To the other side of the world?" he asked so quietly that his mother felt the need to sit closer to him.

"Well, not to the other side of the world, but to the other side of the country. I'm going out West."

It had all happened so fast. At the end of winter, she had applied for a job as an assistant to a landscape artist. Compared to the other job descriptions of the National Park Service, which were quite technical in their requirements, this one was more humanistic, calling for some knowledge of the history of American landscape painting and its European influences. Also, the candidate needed to be a landscape artist herself to do the illustrations for a book on Sequoia and Kings Canyon National Park. The job meant traveling with the writer to the furthermost reaches of that Western expanse. Alice was excited to see that, though the posting specified a one-year contract, the job would be renewable if funding permitted. For her application, Alice wrote an essay that detailed her background in art history and included a series of slides of drawings she had done in Stokes State Forest—trees, brooks, and falls—as well as some photographs she'd taken of the Jersey Shore in winter. She knew it was a long shot and had put it out of her mind, focusing on the portfolio that she needed to complete for graduation. A few weeks later, she was astonished to receive an invitation to meet Ariston Reed, the writer, who happened to be in town, visiting family in Brooklyn.

He was so kind, Alice thought within minutes of their meeting; she rarely had met anyone so gentle. Over lunch, Reed explained the book he was writing—about trees and their particular significance in the varied landscapes of the Park. It would be hard work, traveling through wilderness that was accessible only by foot or on horseback, camping out under the stars, and spending long hours hiking and drawing. Alice daydreamed vividly as he described the Giant

Forest Grove and the sequoia known as General Sherman. At the end of lunch he offered her the job, telling her that her artistic sensibility was just what he was looking for. She heard herself accept, surprised that she could make that big a decision without hesitation. She would have to stick it out, he told her gravely, as her style would really characterize the illustrations and he wanted continuity. Of course, if she was truly homesick—*No chance of that*, she said bluntly. She'd be living amid the tallest trees in the world, the highest mountains, and the deepest caves. She was so smitten by her prospect that she barely heard the last details, something about the National Park Service funding the book and providing food and lodging. Her pay would be pretty low, but she would get 10 percent of the royalties. She signed her contract the following week, wincing when she thought of Adam. It took her a few days to tell the news to her mother because telling Jenna would make it real.

Now staring back into the child's dark and unbelieving eyes, Alice tried to tell him all about the mighty Redwoods in the National Park, but her words fell flat. She reached for his hand; he turned away in search of something to play with. Emma watched him walk away, his step unusually heavy. The women talked about the details of Alice's departure—a week away. It was just as well. A long goodbye would be too hard on Adam; it was too hard already. She couldn't help but feel quite awed by the journey Alice was to make.

As they left the Garden, Adam walked ahead, by himself. Emma thought how odd it was that the ground should be rumbling slightly. She looked around, then realized it wasn't something underground but her own legs that were shaking.

The time had come at last, and yet it still took Emma by surprise. It was early morning, and she was on her way with

Adam to the Green Market in Union Square. As they passed the southeast entrance to Washington Square, she noticed that the iron gate was ajar. Some workers were finally taking down the last of the gratings that had long blocked off the lower triangle of the Square. For three years, Emma had been barred from her diagonal walk through the park from the southeast gate to its opposite point at the northwest corner. And now it was open! She grabbed Adam's hand, and in they went, gazing at the trees that swayed as if in celebration. Adam watched a red-tailed hawk soar above while Emma drank in the expansive greenness of the lawns. It was a paradox almost impossible to sustain: the memory of the trees sacrificed for the renovation haunted the place while the restored fountain—turned on at last—was as festive as fireworks. Its spurts of water sparkled high in the air, then plunged back down, then vanished, then started up again, and yet again. A little girl had taken off her shoes to go wading in the big wet birdbath.

Adam's eyes had been dark all that week. He did little but look through his rock collection or picture books, unable to play with his animal and action figures. He could barely tolerate the presence of Emma or Luke as they sat by him, though glad that they were there. He was quiet during their walk but asked if they might come back to the Square after the market, and if he could play in the fountain. It was the end of May, and the chill was finally gone from the air. Emma thought that she might join him under the giant sprinkler. Adam was soon mesmerized by the hula-hoop girl; the fortune teller, the magician, the mime artist were all back in the green circus.

They made their way to the bright green lawn west of the Arch and stopped for a moment to gaze up into the trees. Their slender, leafy crowns swayed quietly in the wind. It occurred to Emma that in her long preoccupation with the earth, she might be missing out on something essential. Sooner or later she would emerge from those folds. Adam roused her from her daydream, pointing excitedly to a puffy white bird with grey markings in a nearby rhododendron. Mother and child peered into the bush, standing very still so as not to scare the bird away. It hopped down to a lower branch, and Adam ducked down to be eye-level with it. In response, the bird ducked too, cocked its head, and looked right back at Adam, who giggled with delight for the first time in a week.

"I think," Emma whispered, "that's a baby Peregrine Falcon!"

"No, Mom, it's an American Kestrel. I studied them in school."

Emma looked at him with admiration—he was right—and he beamed up at her. But she soon was concerned for that small bird, which seemed to have lost its mother. She roamed the lawn, peering at the sky, which loomed back blankly overhead. She felt like she might cry.

"He'll be okay," Mama. He just fledged a little early."

She reached for Adam's hand, and they walked on. As they approached the gate at the northwest corner he let go, gripped by the majestic sight of the lordly old English elm. He stopped in his tracks; he was sure that he had seen a figure, like a person, in the crook of two big branches, looking down at him. Speechless, he tugged at his Mama's sleeve to point it out to her. But when he looked up again, it was gone.

ABOUT ATMOSPHERE PRESS

Atmosphere Press is an independent, full-service publisher for excellent books in all genres and for all audiences. Learn more about what we do at atmospherepress.com.

We encourage you to check out some of Atmosphere's latest releases, which are available at Amazon.com and via order from your local bookstore:

Dancing with David, a novel by Siegfried Johnson

The Friendship Quilts, a novel by June Calender

My Significant Nobody, a novel by Stevie D. Parker

Nine Days, a novel by Judy Lannon

Shining New Testament: The Cloning of Jay Christ, a novel by Cliff Williamson

Shadows of Robyst, a novel by K. E. Maroudas

Home Within a Landscape, a novel by Alexey L. Kovalev

Motherhood, a novel by Siamak Vakili

Death, The Pharmacist, a novel by D. Ike Horst

Mystery of the Lost Years, a novel by Bobby J. Bixler

Bone Deep Bonds, a novel by B. G. Arnold

Terriers in the Jungle, a novel by Georja Umano

Into the Emerald Dream, a novel by Autumn Allen

His Name Was Ellis, a novel by Joseph Libonati

The Cup, a novel by D. P. Hardwick

The Empathy Academy, a novel by Dustin Grinnell

Tholocco's Wake, a novel by W. W. VanOverbeke

Dying to Live, a novel by Barbara Macpherson Reyelts

Looking for Lawson, a novel by Mark Kirby